The Loves of Lakeside

The Professor

The Loves of Lakeside

The Professor

MIMI FRANCIS

4 Horsemen
Publications, Inc.

4 Horsemen
Publications, Inc.

4 Horsemen Publications, Inc.
1497 Main St. Suite 169
Dunedin, FL 34698
4horsemenpublications.com
info@4horsemenpublications.com

Cover by 4HP
Typeset by Michelle Cline
Editor JM Paquette

Library of Congress Control Number: 2021942120

Print ISBN: 978-1-64450-307-2
Ebook ISBN: 978-1-64450-306-5
Audio ISBN: 978-1-64450-305-8

Table of Contents

Dedication

This one is for my kids. Your support (sometimes reluctant, thanks to the subject matter of my books) means the world to me! Without you, I wouldn't have the guts to follow my dreams. I love you guys!

Chapter 1

Jacob

"Did you know your house is the only one on the street without Christmas lights?" Luke slammed the front door, brushed the snow from his hair, and set the six-pack of beer on the kitchen table.

Jacob rolled his eyes. "I moved in two weeks ago. I don't even *own* Christmas lights. Not to mention, Christmas is a month away. I've got time."

"Add lights to your list." Luke laughed, tipping his head at the fridge, where Jacob had a to-do list for his new home.

Jacob chuckled and shook his head. "Are you gonna help me paint the living room or not? I'd like to unpack some time before the new year."

Luke shucked off his jacket and rolled up his sleeves. He gave his best friend a wry smile before grabbing a beer and heading for the living room. Jacob followed him.

It had been less than two weeks since he'd moved into his new place, and Jacob was still living out of boxes. He wanted to get some remodeling done before the second semester of school started. He suspected he wouldn't have much time once he went to work.

"Have you talked to Charlie?" Luke asked. He was on the ladder, edging the wall with paint below the ceiling; Luke had a steadier hand than Jacob, so he'd willingly given up the job to his best friend.

"His assistant called me. Serena, right?"

Luke nodded. "Yeah. She's sweet and new to town. Moved here in the fall, I think. Her boyfriend is the head of campus security. Nice guy. Evan something. Him and his friend own some big security company back east. What did she say?"

"Everything's ready. They set my classes and delivered my stuff to my office last week. Everybody is so excited to have me at Lakeside. Blah, blah, blah."

Luke stepped off the ladder and poked him in the shoulder. "What's wrong?"

Jacob scrubbed a hand over his face, scratching at the growing facial hair. He hadn't decided if he was going to keep the beard or not. He kind of liked it, and knowing his dad would have approved made keeping it even more appealing. He sighed and dropped to the tarp-covered couch.

"I never wanted to come back to Lakeside," he said. "I thought when I left for college, I was leaving it behind forever. Coming back is like admitting defeat."

"Seriously?" Luke chuckled. "You're one of the foremost experts in your field. How many people from our high school got a doctorate before they were twenty-five? Not one of them is a certified genius. Where's your Mensa card by the way? If I were you, I would frame it on my goddamn office door right beside my doctorate. We should call you Dr. Moore instead of Professor Moore."

Jacob scoffed. "Dr. Moore sounds so pompous. I'll stick with Professor Moore."

"Coming home isn't a failure, Jake. Maybe it was time. You spent the last three years hiding in Rome—"

"I wasn't hiding. I was working."

Luke grinned. "You're full of shit. You were hiding from Maggie."

"And I'm not hiding now?" Jacob wondered. "Coming home isn't running away from Rome and Gianna?"

"Is it?" Luke asked gently. "Or did you finally realize this is where you belong? It sucks your dad's death brought you back, but you're here now. You should make the best of it. After everything with Maggie and then Gianna—"

He rolled his eyes. "Can we talk about something else? Please?"

"Sure." An evil grin spread across Luke's face. Jacob didn't like it at all. "Are you ready to date? It's been, what, two months since you got back? Now that you're home, maybe it's time to find a new woman."

"You make it sound as easy as buying a new pair of shoes." Jacob sighed.

Luke laughed. "I'm not saying it's easy. I know it's not. But you could at least try."

"I wouldn't even know where to start."

"You don't have to find someone to marry. Just someone to date and have fun with." He smirked. "You know, I bet Bonnie has a friend." Luke took a sip of his beer and stared at his friend.

"I don't want to be set up."

"Just hear me out. Go out for drinks with me, Bonnie, and one of her single friends. We can go to Time Out, have a drink, maybe play some pool. Just friends hanging out, nothing more. It'll do you good to get out of the house. You need to quit moping around."

"I enjoy moping," Jacob grumbled.

Luke rolled his eyes and threw a roll of painter's tape at him. Jacob burst out laughing.

"I'll tell you what: I'll think about it, okay?" Jacob said. "At least let me get through the first few weeks of the semester, and then we'll talk about it."

"I'm considering that a promise. And I'm holding you to it."

Jacob ignored the remark, picked up a can of paint, and held it out to his best friend. "Finish the wall so I can unpack before Christmas gets here."

———

The wind stung his cheeks and nose, making his face burn and his eyes water. Each breath hurt and made his lungs ache. He forgot how cold it got in Montana. Winters in Rome were mild, rainy, and it rarely snowed; winters in Montana were like a punch to the gut. He regretted venturing out of his office in search of coffee. But the student union was closed for winter break, and Jacob was forced to find a place off-campus. Wet, thick snow grew heavier as he walked across campus, chilling his bones in seconds.

Jacob yanked open the door of the first cafe he came across—a small coffee shop near the university. It had been a burger place the last time he'd been in town.

The place was deserted—all the tables empty. He took a second to stomp the snow from his boots and shoved his gloves in his coat pocket before he cleared his throat, hoping to get someone's attention.

A young woman emerged from the back wearing a black apron and a name tag he couldn't read. She was short—maybe 5'4" or 5'5", much shorter than his 6'2"—with long, blonde hair and big, warm, chocolate brown eyes. Voluptuous, curvaceous, *gorgeous*. She plastered a smile on her face as he turned toward her, one of those *I-work-in-customer-service-so-I-have-to-be-here-and-pretend-I-like-it* smiles. Her eyes widened when she saw him, and he heard her sharp intake of breath. Jacob chuckled under his breath.

"H-hi," she stammered. "C-can I help you?"

"Can I get a cup of coffee while I wait for the snow to stop?" he asked, pointing over his shoulder at the burgeoning blizzard.

She leaned to the side and peered out the window. "Wow, it's really coming down. Um, sure. Just coffee? How do you take it?"

"Black, no cream, one sugar."

She grabbed a cup, filled it to the brim, and dropped in a packet of sugar, snapping the lid on and wiping the sides before handing it to him. He held out the cash, but she waved it away.

"On the house." A genuine smile lit up her face.

His heart thudded at the sight, and his breath caught in his throat. He propped a hip against the counter and gave her his best smile.

"You always give free coffee to strangers?" Jacob asked.

"Only the attractive ones," she quipped, the smile now accompanied by a flirty wink.

He laughed and shook his head. He was aware of the effect he had on others—he taught many classes filled with young men and women who were not always subtle about their attraction to him. Over the years, he'd learned to ignore it. The stares, the giggling, the blatant innuendos, even the occasional inappropriate social media post—he'd dealt with all of them over the years. He'd learned to close himself off and only let a few people in, like Luke. Those walls had protected him from any more heartbreak. But something about this girl made him want to break down those walls with a goddamn sledgehammer.

He stared; he couldn't help it. She was stunning with her full pink lips, the blonde hair skimming her waist, full breasts, and an impressive body, obvious even under her oversized sweatshirt and dowdy black apron.

"I'm Jacob." He held out his hand. "And you are?"

Chapter 2

Avery

$\mathcal{S}$he stared up at the insanely gorgeous man exuding masculinity. He wasn't like any of the boys she knew. He was all man. He wore clean, pressed jeans and a wrinkle-free, red plaid button up under his soft, brown leather jacket. He had on work boots, unscuffed and clean. His light brown hair was short and neat, spiked in the front, and he had a well-kept beard, short and neat like he'd grown it during the last couple of weeks. A light dusting of freckles covered his cheeks below a set of gorgeous emerald green eyes and a mouth that could stop traffic. Full, pink, utterly kissable lips. Heart-stopping, distracting lips. Avery imagined those lips wrapped around her—

Too late, she realized she was staring and biting her lip, lost in the fantasy playing in her head—a fantasy involving her, him, and a private room with a big, soft bed. He said something that she missed, too busy daydreaming. A smirk tugged at the corner of his mouth.

"I-I'm sorry. What was that?"

"I said I'm Jacob. Then I asked your name." He dropped his hand and smiled again, crinkles forming at the corners of his sparkling, green eyes.

"Avery," she blurted. "My name is Avery." She looked away, heat blooming in her cheeks. *God, is there anything about this man that isn't sexy?* His voice was deep and rich, the sound shaking her to the core. She took a sip of the tea she'd stashed under the counter and tried to look anywhere but those damn green eyes. They drew her in and wouldn't let her go.

"Nice to meet you, Avery," Jacob said. He raised his coffee cup in a salute. "Thanks for this. I'm gonna hang out over there until the snow stops." He made his way to a table facing the window and took a seat.

Avery took another swallow of tea and burned her tongue. *I'm an idiot. And out of touch. Guys used to beg to take me out and offered the world on a silver platter.*

She chastised herself as she cleaned up behind the counter, getting ready for the next shift to come in. Once she had everything the way Ruby liked it, she slipped onto the stool behind the counter and stared out the window. She wanted to gaze at the handsome stranger in the corner, but she thought it might be creepy. It didn't stop her earlier fantasy from playing out in her head, her imagination in overdrive, her internal temperature rising with every scenario.

"Excuse me?"

Jacob stood in front of her. Busted again. She exhaled and smiled.

"Yes, sir?"

"I was wondering if you'd like to go out some time. Maybe grab some coffee or something?"

Avery snorted and rolled her eyes. It wasn't until she shot a glance around the coffee shop that Jacob realized what he'd said. He let loose a full, booming laugh. Avery's skin tingled.

"Okay, so I bombed that." He chuckled. He shrugged a shoulder and gave her a sheepish grin. "Forget I said anything." He yanked his gloves from his coat pocket and turned to go.

"I'd love to go out with you," Avery said, stopping him in his tracks.

Jacob turned and gave her a brilliant smile. He crossed the room in two strides and scribbled his number on the back of one of the paper menus. "I'll leave it up to you. If you decide I wasn't a total idiot, call me. If you think I'm insane, and you never want to see me again, toss it in the trash when I leave."

She giggled and took the menu from him. "Seems like a reasonable request."

His eyes sparkled, and his smile lit up the room. "I'll talk to you soon." He walked backward until he got to the door then winked at her. "I hope."

———

Avery hung her apron in the back, said goodbye to Jules and Ruby, and left without mentioning Jacob to either of them. She kept that information to herself, eager to get home and relax. She'd worked a double shift at the coffee shop by herself. Her body weighed a thousand pounds, her feet ached, and her head pounded. She needed food and sleep, in that order.

Her boss, Ruby, owned two locations of The Percolator in Lakeside, and Avery had worked at both since moving to town five years ago. When she moved out of the dorms at the university and into her own apartment, she started working at the one near the university, putting in as many hours as possible. It was within walking distance of her apartment and school, so she kept her car maintenance bill low, a necessity since she wasn't sure her crappy sedan would last until she graduated.

It took her ten minutes to walk home—her fingers and toes frozen by the time she closed the apartment door behind her. She stripped off her work clothes, put on her warmest pajamas—pants, a sweatshirt, and fuzzy socks—before settling on the couch with a heavy quilt. Fortunately, Nat wasn't home; she'd gone to Great Falls with her boyfriend for the holidays and wouldn't be back until the second semester. Avery let her mind drift to Jacob and whether she should take him up on his offer.

She hadn't dated in a while, not since Brent. After high school, unsure what she wanted to do with her life, she'd taken a year off and spent most of her time drinking and partying. One night, she woke up in a strange apartment with no idea where she was or who she was with, and it scared the crap out of her. She vowed to get her life together. She'd left Missoula, moved north to Lakeside, and enrolled at the university.

The change of scenery did nothing to stem her bad habits; she continued partying, rarely attended class, and scraped by with her grades. Avery came to her senses when Ruby sat her down and gave her an earful about her atrocious behavior. She quit drinking, stopped partying, and curbed her bad dating habits. No more frat boys, no more men she needed to tame. No more sex for the sake of sex. The last date she had was the end of her junior year, a blind date with a friend of a friend, one of the sheriff's deputies. She went on four or five dates with Brent before they agreed to end it.

Jacob was a temptation she couldn't afford. She had five months until graduation. She had to keep it together and forget the man that had consumed her thoughts since he walked into the coffee shop. She couldn't figure him out.

Jacob didn't look like a college student—he was too sophisticated and put together. He wasn't a local or a professor at the college. After living in Lakeside for the last five years, she knew most of the townies and people who worked at Lakeside University.

Locals, college students, and university faculty filled the town. College students were easy to spot—young, frantic, and stressed—while the locals had a perpetual look of reluctant acceptance. She couldn't blame them; summer brought the tourists, and the rest of the year they dealt with the constant influx of young adults learning their place in the world. The residents of Lakeside were undeniably patient.

Jacob was definitely a mystery. She had yet to decide if she wanted to unravel him.

———

Avery parked in the lot behind the coffee shop, yanked open the back door, and hurried through the kitchen, waving at Jules and her friend Carson before she darted into the employee bathroom to check her hair and makeup. Satisfied with what she saw, Avery went to the front counter and made herself a large vanilla latte. She looked around for Jacob.

It had taken her less than thirty minutes to call him and agree to a date. Their first phone call lasted almost an hour, and over the past several days, they'd texted and talked several times. She'd been looking forward to their date all week.

She had one slight panicky moment on the drive over, wondering if she made a mistake by agreeing to a date with someone she barely knew. But ignoring the little naysayer in her head, she'd crossed her fingers and hoped for the best.

Jacob sat in the back, in front of the large windows overlooking the university, jotting notes in a leather-bound notebook propped in his lap. He wore jeans again and the same work boots, along with a plain white button-down and a black blazer. He gnawed on his lower lip, concentrating on his writing.

Avery poured him a cup of coffee—no cream, one sugar—and crossed the restaurant, clearing her throat as she approached the table.

"Hi," she mumbled. Her stomach churned, and her hands shook. Men never intimidated her, never scared her. She always held the upper hand with them, but being in Jacob's presence made her feel as if she were walking on uneven ground. She didn't like it.

"Hey." He smiled, rose to his feet, and pulled out a chair for her.

She set the steaming mug on the table, sat down, and folded her hands on the tabletop.

"Thanks," he said. "You didn't have to—"

Avery waved his protest away with one hand. "I know the owner."

Jacob's laugh sent a tingle of desire down her spine. Even his laugh was sexy. She dragged in a deep breath and smiled at him.

I have nothing to worry about! Things will be fine.

Chapter 3
Jacob

Jacob enjoyed spending time with Avery. She was funny, smart, and stunning. Their relationship was uncomplicated—two people having fun. They went bowling, played pool at Time Out, tried ice skating in the park, and even caught a movie at the small theater downtown. It was exactly what Jacob needed. He felt normal for the first time since he left Rome. The weeks before second semester flew by.

The Saturday before the semester started, he invited Avery over for dinner—pizza from Roselli's. It had been three weeks since their first date and things were going well.

Avery's small, yellow sedan was parked in front of his house when he rounded the corner. He'd hoped to get back before she arrived, but the pizza place was packed, the line going out the door. By the time he got back to his place, it was almost dark.

He would have been on time, but Charlie Ross, the university president, called to ask him a favor. One of the other professors in Jacob's department, Walter Hess, had a family emergency and had to go home to Iowa. Charlie didn't know how long he would be gone, but Hess would miss several weeks of the second semester. Charlie begged Jacob to take on one of his senior level classes. It was too late to cancel it.

Jacob agreed. He wasn't teaching a full load this semester, only three freshman classes, so taking on another class wasn't a big deal. Charlie had been extremely grateful.

"If you need anything, Jacob, let me know. I mean it: anything."

He hit the garage door opener and turned into the driveway. Avery climbed from her car and waited outside, watching as he stepped out of his car.

"You're late."

"Hello to you, too." He smirked. "I got a late start, and the pizza place was packed."

"Roselli's? Yeah, they're always busy, especially before school starts. All the college kids are back in town. I guess I should have warned you." She shifted the bag she carried to her other arm.

"What's in there?" Jacob asked, nodding at the bag.

"Wine. And salad."

"Well, quit lurking in the driveway and get in here." He yanked open the passenger side door and pulled out the pizzas.

Jacob led Avery into the house and kitchen, set the pizzas on the table, and tossed his backpack into the corner. He showed her where he kept the plates and glasses then went to clean up. By the time he returned to the kitchen, Avery had set the table and poured the wine.

Avery leaned against the counter, staring out the window into his backyard, her lower lip caught between her teeth. He stopped beside her, rested his hand on the center of her back, and pressed a kiss to her cheek. She smiled up at him.

"Hi," she breathed. She wrapped her fingers in the front of his sweater, pushed up on her toes, and kissed him, her lips lingering on his. Desire twisted in his gut.

"Hi." His arm snaked around her waist, holding her close. "You hungry?"

"Starving."

Jacob laughed. "Me, too." He kissed her again and reluctantly pulled away. "Your choices are supreme or ham with pineapple. And if you make fun of my love of fruit on pizza, we are going to have a problem."

Avery's grin lit up her face. "You just sealed the deal. Ham and pineapple is my favorite."

"I knew you were the perfect woman." He winked and pulled out the kitchen chair with a flourish. "Have a seat."

After dinner, they cleaned up the kitchen, then Avery insisted on a tour. Jacob put his arm around her waist and led her through the house, pointing out the areas he wanted to remodel.

She paused outside his office, her eyes on the wall behind his desk. She stepped out of the circle of his arms and walked inside, coming to a stop in front of his desk.

"Jacob, what do you do for a living?" she asked.

It was a question she'd never asked him. In fact, they never talked about his work—it never came up. It hadn't seemed important.

"I'm a professor at the university."

Avery's shoulders slumped, and she shook her head. She muttered something indiscernible under her breath and turned to him. "At Lakeside? You're a professor at Lakeside University?"

"Yes. Avery, what's wrong?"

"I'm a student at Lakeside, Jacob." She shifted back a step and crossed her arms over her chest.

Jacob's head spun. He dropped into his desk chair and put his head in his hands. "Well, shit."

"That's all you have to say?" Avery snapped. "Well, shit?"

"I...I don't know what to say." He sighed. "I didn't know you were a student."

Avery's eyes narrowed, and her lips pursed. "You could have asked. You never did."

Jacob slapped the desk and rose to his feet. "Jesus, Avery, give me a break." He rubbed the back of his neck. "You don't look or act like a student. You're a wo—" His mouth snapped shut, and he closed his eyes. "How old are you anyway?"

"I'm twenty-five," she replied. "And you're right: I don't look like a student. I'm a senior. I graduate in May. I started college late and took things slow." She ran a hand through her hair, holding it off her neck. "I'm sorry. I shouldn't have snapped at you."

"It's alright. I'm sorry, too." He stepped around his desk and caught her hand. "Are you okay?"

"No." She shrugged. "I like you, Jacob. A lot. These last few weeks, spending time with you, it's been great. I thought maybe we—you and me—maybe we could...I don't know, I guess I thought there was something there, something between us. Don't you feel it, too?"

"I did. I *do*." He rubbed a hand up and down her arm. "But if you're a student—"

Avery took a step back, distancing herself from him. "But if I'm a student...what?"

"Avery, I could...I could lose my job. Dating a student, it's...well, it's wrong."

She laughed—a bitter, disdainful thing that hurt his head. "So, that's it then? Three weeks of fun and it's over?"

Jacob didn't know what to say. Being with Avery made him happier than he'd been since he moved to Rome. But he couldn't give up his job and everything he'd worked for to pursue a student. He just couldn't.

He opened his mouth, closed it, and settled for shrugging his shoulders. He didn't know what to say. Avery squared her shoulders and spun on her heels. She disappeared out the office door. A few seconds later, his front door slammed.

Chapter 4

Avery

You're so stupid, Avery. How did you think you could have a relationship with a guy like Jacob?

His silence screamed his answer and told her everything she needed to know. She was a student, and he was a professor—it couldn't happen. *They* couldn't happen. It was better to leave than endure another minute with a man she couldn't have.

She hadn't expected anything to come out of their relationship, but the hope had been there. She liked Jacob; they connected in a way she'd never experienced before. The last three weeks had been fun and, she'd hoped, the beginning of something great. When she walked into his office and saw the diplomas and the books written by Dr. Jacob Moore, her stomach dropped to her toes.

"Over before it started," she muttered under her breath, swiping unnecessary tears from her cheeks. She swung into her parking space and hurried inside her apartment.

Nat wouldn't be back until tomorrow, so Avery had the apartment to herself. She took advantage, throwing on her favorite ratty pajamas and pouring a large glass of wine. A cheesy movie on the television made her feel a little better. She rested her head on the back of the couch and stared at the ceiling.

How did I not know Jacob was a professor?

She replayed every conversation they'd had the last few weeks, desperate to find a clue he might have given her. Nothing came to mind.

Avery picked up her battered laptop from the table. Her fingers hovered over the keys, her heart and head arguing with each other. *Let it go. Move on. Forget he existed.* Instead, she typed his name in the search engine.

Professor Moore—Dr. Moore—was thirty years old; he'd gone to college when he was seventeen. By the time he was twenty-four, he had his doctorate. He was a certified genius, a card-carrying member of Mensa. He spent the last five years in Italy, teaching anthropology at Sapienza Universita di Roma. Avery discovered he was one of the most well-known figures in his field, a feat rarely accomplished by someone his age. There were rumors he'd been engaged while he lived in Italy, though she couldn't find any other information about it. He did a good job of keeping his private life offline. Two months ago, his father died. Now he was back in Lakeside, his hometown.

Avery had no idea he was from Lakeside. He seemed so sophisticated. Shit, he was more sophisticated than anyone she knew in Montana. She wondered if anyone had known Jacob when he lived here before. It couldn't hurt to ask around.

Around midnight, she closed her laptop. Her eyes burned, and her head pounded. After looking up everything she could about Jacob, she took a chance and pulled up the employee handbook for the university. She clung to the hope that since Jacob wasn't her teacher, they could still see each other. She searched for over an hour but found nothing.

Avery dumped the rest of her wine in the sink and went to bed, vowing to forget about the handsome professor and the fun they'd had. She fell asleep with his laughter ringing in her ears.

—

Her last class on Monday—the first day of her final semester of college—was on the other side of campus, the farthest building from student parking.

As she hurried across the grounds, the chill in the air seeped into her bones, and her thoughts turned again to Jacob. He'd been constantly on her mind. Since dating him was forbidden—or likely forbidden—he became even more appealing. For the last two nights, she tossed and turned, unable to get him out of her head. He was driving her crazy.

Jacob left her brain as she stepped through the classroom door. It was nearly full, only a few empty seats scattered around the room. She sighed and made her way down a middle aisle, slipping into a seat in the center of the room.

"BILINGUALISM IN SOCIAL CONTEXT" was written across the old-fashioned chalkboard. Avery didn't see the professor anywhere, not that she would recognize Professor Hess anyway. She'd never been in one of his classes before this year; Hess only taught upper classmen and graduate classes. According to rumor, his class would be the most difficult she was taking this semester.

The door at the top of the stairs slamming closed pulled her from her thoughts. She glanced at the clock above the chalkboard. Looked like Professor Hess was tardy to his own class.

"Sorry about that, guys," a deep, familiar voice called. "Sucks to be late when you're the teacher."

Avery sat bolt upright, realization slamming into her. She turned to see Jacob striding down the stairs, an army green backpack slung over his shoulder. He wore a dark blue peacoat over a hunter green button up, jeans cuffed over his work boots. He looked phenomenal. Jacob dropped his backpack to the floor, tossed his coat onto the chair, pushed up his sleeves, and propped a hip on the wooden desk. He smiled at the class assembled in front of him.

"As some of you may know, I am *not* Professor Hess." A collective laugh echoed around the room and Jacob smiled. He hopped off the desk, crossed to the chalkboard, and wrote "Professor Moore" beneath the course name. "I will be teaching Bilingualism in Social Context for the next few weeks while Professor Hess attends to some personal matters. Hopefully, you guys don't mind putting up with me."

Another laugh filled the room, this one heavy on female giggles. Avery rolled her eyes and slumped in her seat. Maybe Jacob wouldn't notice her.

Sheer force of will propelled Avery to pick up her pen and follow along while Jacob lectured, going over the syllabus. He paced around the front of the room like a caged tiger—animated, excited, and unbelievably sexy—his green eyes bright with excitement and his smile dazzling the entire room.

Avery watched him in awe, frustrated and astonished that the world put the one off-limits man in Lakeside in front of her again.

Chapter 5

Jacob

Jacob spent Sunday at the university unpacking, organizing his office, and trying to get Avery out of his head.

It was stupid of him to not ask Avery if she was a student. He should have known better, living in a town filled with college students. But he'd been intentionally ignorant because Avery captured his attention like no one else. Being with her was uncomplicated and fun. He missed that in his life and didn't want to think about anything else.

It wasn't until his stomach rumbled that he looked at the clock on the wall. He'd been at it all day; he needed food and something to drink.

There was a burrito and a cold beer in his fridge at home, not to mention a comfortable bed. Maybe a good night's sleep would help him forget about the petite blonde with the chocolate brown eyes consuming his every thought. He grabbed his jacket, gathered some books from the table, and turned to go.

Margaret "Maggie" Hudspeth leaned against the door jamb, hip jutted out, examining her long red nails. She was something else. Tall, brunette, with a set of tits that would turn a dead man's head and deep blue eyes one could drown in. It was easy to see why he'd fallen for her all those years ago.

"Jacob," she purred. "It's good to see you."

"Mags."

"Nobody has called me that since you moved." She pushed past him, walking into his office like she owned the place. She went straight to his beat up couch and sat down, her long legs crossed at the ankles, a tight smile on her face.

"How are you doing?" Maggie asked.

He shrugged. "I'm okay." He set the books and his jacket on the desk.

"I was sorry to hear about your dad."

"Thank you," Jacob said.

Maggie cleared her throat. "You've been in town for what? Two months? You couldn't call or email or something? I have to show up in your office uninvited to get you to talk to me."

"Do you even want to talk to me, Mags? After everything that happened?"

"I'm here, aren't I? Besides, it was a long time ago. Things are different now."

Jacob eased into the chair across from Maggie. "True. How are you?"

She raised a shoulder, her eyes fixed on something behind him. "Not bad."

When Maggie lied, she refused to look him in the eye. It was how he'd known they shouldn't get married; she said "I love you" but hadn't looked at him. Her eyes told him the truth.

"Hm." He clasped his hands between his legs and got to the point. "Why are you here, Mags?"

"Can't I come say hello to an old friend? My former fiancé?"

Maggie never did anything without a reason. Jacob leaned back and crossed his arms. "Spill it."

Maggie rolled her eyes. "I hate it when you do that." She cleared her throat. "I want to know why you've been avoiding me."

"I didn't think you'd want to talk to me, Maggie. You said some harsh things when we split up. I believe one of them was 'I hate you and I never want to see you again.' Or am I wrong?"

Maggie shook her head. "No, you're not wrong. I said that. But I would like to reiterate that it was a long time ago, and things have changed. I'm not the same person I was when we broke up. You're not the only person who got out of this godforsaken town."

"Oh?"

"After you left, I moved to Denver. I taught high school for two years and a couple of community college classes. Getting away gave me some perspective."

"But you came back, like I did. How come?" Jake questioned.

"Ross offered me a job. Called and asked me to teach Science," she explained. "So, here I am. Like I said, I'm not the same person I was after our breakup. I doubt you are either."

Jacob nodded. "I'm not the same person. But I still don't understand why you're here."

"I wanted to see you, talk to you, and tell you I forgive you."

Jacob shifted uneasily. He hadn't expected this, maybe anger or disinterest, but not forgiveness. He scrubbed a hand over his face.

Maggie smirked. "Surprised?"

"You don't hate me?"

"I did for a long time. Until I realized our break-up was a good thing. For both of us. We were too young to get married. Neither one of us knew what we wanted or where our lives were going. I have no regrets, and I don't hate you." Maggie leaned forward, her elbows on her jean-clad legs, her tits on full display. "Do you forgive me? I said a lot of hateful things to and about you. Things I regret now."

Jacob forced himself to focus on her face. "Like you said, it's all in the past."

"Can we start over?" Maggie murmured.

There it was. His ex-fiancée was never subtle. She wanted something. He cleared his throat.

"What do you mean 'start over,' Mags?"

She sighed. "We could get dinner some time. Catch up?"

How the hell was he supposed to respond? If he told her no, old hateful feelings might resurface. But he couldn't tell her yes; he suspected she wanted more, and he didn't. He wasn't sure he'd ever want anything with Maggie. Their time had come and gone.

"Maybe." Jacob shrugged, hoping his noncommittal answer would dissuade her from pursuing the issue. "Look, I need to get home, get some rest before tomorrow."

"Of course," Maggie said, her eyes narrow and lips pursed. "I'll go." She rose to her feet, reached into her jacket, and pulled out a card. She set it on the coffee table in front of him. "Call me when you want to grab dinner."

Jacob watched her sashay from the room, her hands in her pockets, shoulders back, tall and proud.

What do you really want, Mags?

———

By the time Jacob's last class of the day rolled around—the class he'd agreed to teach until Hess returned—he was exhausted. He hadn't slept well the night before—nerves kept him up, and he spent the evening talking himself out of calling Avery.

He had office hours before Hess's class, but since classes had just started, he was free to get coffee. He needed the caffeine. In the student union, he ran into Luke, who insisted on hearing all about his first day. Jacob lost track of time and sprinted across campus, not making it to class until four minutes after the hour.

"Sorry," he muttered as he jogged down the stairs. "Sucks to be late when you're the teacher." He dropped his backpack on the floor next to the desk, threw his coat on the chair, leaned against the desk, and smiled at the assembled students.

Jacob loved teaching more than anything. He got a thrill out of sharing knowledge with his students and loved seeing the light in their eyes. And the first day of a new class was his favorite. It always seemed to go by in a blur of faces, voices, and questions—some of it not sinking in until long after class ended. Even though it was his last class of the day, and a class he would only teach for a few weeks, he was on a roll, the words coming easily as he paced across the front of the classroom, gesturing like crazy.

Class was almost over before he noticed Avery in the center of the class, slumped in her seat. He had taken the class syllabus and ran up the stairs, dropping a stack at the head of each row. When he stopped in front of the class, his eyes locked on hers. His gut twisted.

How did I not notice her before?

Jacob cleared his throat and clapped his hands together. "Sorry again for being late. I won't make a habit of it if you don't. Read through the syllabus, email me, or stop by during office hours if you have questions. We'll jump right in next class and get started. I expect everyone to be prepared."

He kept an eye on Avery as the other students filed out of the room. Several of them stopped to ask him questions—no surprise on the first day. Avery took her time putting her things in her bag, watching him out of the corner of her eye. The door closed behind the last student. She meandered down the stairs and stopped a safe distance away from him.

"Hi," he said. His damn hands shook, and his heart pounded painfully.

"Hello," she replied. She pushed a hand through her blonde curls, shoving them from her face. "I can't believe you're teaching this class."

"It's temporary, Avery. Only until Hess gets back." He spun around, entered his office, shoved the chair away from the desk, and dropped into it.

Avery followed him—small, angry, and irritated. She slammed the door closed and paced in a circle in front of him, her hair whipping around her face every time she spun around. "I'd drop it if I didn't need it to graduate. How am I supposed to sit here every day with you teaching the class? It's not fair."

Jacob leaned forward, his elbows on his knees. "You're right. It isn't fair."

"I'm so glad you agree with me," she mumbled. She stopped in front of his desk, crossed her arms, and glared at him. "How can you sit there and do nothing?"

Jacob rubbed a hand over his nape. He straightened his shoulders and locked eyes with Avery. His head spun. "I don't know what you want me to do, Avery. I like you. A lot. There was something between us, something special."

Avery's eyes dropped to the ground, and she sighed. "I thought so, too. I guess we'll never know, will we? I should go." She yanked her bag higher onto her shoulder, sighed, and pivoted to leave.

Jacob shot out of his chair and lunged across the room. He grabbed her elbow, but when he opened his mouth, what came out was not at all what he expected.

"I don't want you to go. I want this. I want us," he whispered into her ear. Clean strawberry and vanilla fragrance wafted from her skin, filling his head. He closed his eyes and forced himself to concentrate. "Don't go. Stay here and talk to me."

Avery turned her head, their breath mingling as the air between them thickened with desire.

He wanted this woman, wanted to touch her, to kiss her, to do so much more to her. It didn't matter that she was a student or that he'd only known her a few weeks, not when she was inches away from him. So close, so tempting.

Jacob ducked his head and caught her lips with his. He hadn't felt like this in years. It was insane, the burning need coursing through his veins and overriding all rational thought. His arms slid around her waist and pulled her tight against his body. Her arms came up around his neck, her bag falling to the floor. She moaned in his mouth, the sound a punch to his gut.

"Professor Moore?"

The voice drifting through the closed door startled them and forced them apart. Jacob groaned, disappointment flooding him as he let her go and took several steps back. He cleared his throat and waited a heartbeat, trying to catch his breath. Grumbling to himself, he adjusted his shirt to hide his arousal.

"Stay here," he whispered. He stalked across the room, yanked open the door, and pulled it closed behind him.

The university president stood in the middle of Jacob's classroom. His smile widened when Jacob stepped out of his office.

"Mr. Ross? How are you?"

"I'm doing well," Charlie replied. "I stopped by to see how your first day was."

Jacob smiled. "It was great."

"I'd love to hear about it. Why don't you come to my office, and we can chat?"

"Sounds great. Let me gather my stuff. I can be there in ten minutes."

"Fantastic. I'll see you then."

Jacob waited until Charlie left the room before he returned to his office. Avery sat on the couch, her bag on the floor between her feet. Her cheeks were a delicate pink, and her chest heaved with deep breaths.

"I have to go," he said. "Can I call you later?"

Avery nodded and rose to her feet, her bag clutched in her hands. She walked past him without a word.

Chapter 6

Avery

Avery's mind reeled. She kissed her professor, and Charles Ross, the university president, almost saw. Despite the cold of the January afternoon, sweat dripped down her back. Avery slipped the ever-present ponytail holder from her wrist and pulled her long blonde hair into a messy bun. She kept her eyes down, praying she wouldn't run into anyone while her brain was spinning out of control. She sprinted across the parking lot and slid to a stop next to her car.

Fumbling with the door handle, her nail caught on it and broke. Tears filled her eyes, and she cursed under her breath. She opened the door, threw herself inside, and shoved the key in the ignition. The car sputtered to life.

Five minutes later, she parked on the street in front of her building and hurried inside. She sprinted up three flights to her apartment, burst through the door, and ran right into her roommate Natasha.

"Hey, whoa," Nat gasped, stumbling backward and catching herself on a kitchen chair. "You okay?"

"No," Avery snapped. "I mean, yes. I guess. Sorry." She pushed past her and into her bedroom, slamming the door behind her.

She slumped on the edge of the bed, her bag falling to the floor with a loud clunk, and dropped her head into her hands. Everything was happening so fast. She was going insane. There was something about Professor Moore that drew her in like a moth to a flame. Avery had never been with anyone who made her want to throw all the rules out the window. She wanted to see him again, kiss him again, touch him again.

At least she didn't have class with Jacob—*Professor Moore* she reminded herself—until Wednesday. Bilingualism in Social Context met four days a week: Monday, Wednesday, Thursday, and Friday for an hour and a half. It would give her time to figure out what she was going to do.

She pressed her fingers to her lips, her eyes slipping closed as she recalled the kiss they'd shared. It held such promise. She'd gotten her hopes up, forgetting for a moment Jacob was a professor and she was his student. Things couldn't go any further between them.

———

An hour later, she emerged from the bedroom, determined to take her mind off Professor Jacob Moore. Maybe hanging out with Nat would help.

"Hey, stranger," Nat giggled. She jumped off the couch and hugged Avery a little too tightly.

The tiny redhead was a ball of energy, exhausting Avery with her positive attitude. She loved her roommate and best friend despite her nosiness and unending stream of over-the-top vivacity.

"How are your classes?" Nat asked.

Avery grabbed a bottle of water from the fridge and dropped to the couch beside Nat. "They're okay. Too early to tell."

"Do you have the new professor? Professor Moore? God, everyone is talking about him."

"He's teaching Hess's class for a few weeks," Avery said. Unexpected jealousy twisted in her gut.

"Is he as gorgeous as everyone says?" Nat asked.

"He is insanely handsome. Like stop-dead-in-your-tracks-to-stare-at-him handsome."

"You're so lucky!" Nat squealed. "I'd give anything to sit in class and stare at him all day. I guess he moved here from Rome because he was heartbroken or something. Did you know he's from here? Rumor has it he used to date Professor Hudspeth in the Science department when they were in high school. It wouldn't surprise me if they started dating again. Like a rebound thing."

Nat talked so fast it hurt Avery's head. She hadn't heard the rumors about Jacob. Or she hadn't been listening. She'd been in her headspace all day, upset over the loss of her relationship with Jacob and worried about her classes. She should have been listening.

Nat prattled on, even after Avery's phone chimed with an incoming message. She snuck a peek at it.

[Jacob: Meet me for a drink?]

With a sigh she hoped her roommate didn't notice, she picked up her phone and flicked her finger across the screen, keeping it out of Nat's eyeline.

[Avery: Are you sure that's a good idea?]

[Jacob: I just want to talk. Please?]

Avery squeezed the phone so tightly she was surprised it didn't break. *God, I want to say yes, but one of us has to be smart and do the right thing.* The phone chimed again.

[Jacob: Avery? Please?]

She closed her eyes, dragged in a deep breath, then exhaled slowly. She stared at the wall above Nat's head but didn't see the pale-yellow wallpaper with faded pink flowers. She saw Jacob's face smiling at her.

[Avery: Okay. Where?]

———

Nat gave her the third degree about where she was going and who she was seeing, but Avery refused to answer, telling her roommate it was private. Fortunately, a phone call from Nat's boyfriend, Brick, interrupted the interrogation and allowed Avery to sneak away.

An hour after Jacob's text, she stood outside Brannigan's Pub in Kalispell, twenty minutes north of Lakeside. Jacob suggested it. It was unlikely students or staff from the university would be there, especially on a Monday night. Avery saw Jacob through the window, sitting at a table with a beer in front of him.

She contemplated turning around and going home, ending it before it began. Instead, she yanked off her hat, her blonde hair tumbling around her shoulders, and stepped inside.

"Avery!" Jacob called.

She eased into the seat across from him with an uneasy smile. "Hi, Jacob."

"Thank you for coming." He grinned. "Do you want something to drink?" He waved at the server.

"Can I get a sparkling wine?"

Jacob ordered her drink, sat back in his chair, and tapped his fingers on the table. Avery didn't know what to say or how to act. What was the proper etiquette for a pseudo-date with one's professor?

The server returned with her drink and a plate of the pub's infamous black and tan onion rings. She sipped her wine and shifted in her seat.

"This is weird, huh?" Jacob said, picking at the corner of his napkin.

"Yeah, a little." She sighed. "Or a lot." A nervous giggle escaped her.

He reached across the table and took her hand, intertwining his fingers with hers. "I don't want to lie to you, Avery. I'm attracted to you. I haven't felt like this since—" His mouth snapped shut, and he cleared his throat. "It's been a long time."

"I'm your student, Jacob." She pulled her hand from his.

Jacob sighed and folded his hands in front of him. "Only because I'm teaching Hess's class. If I weren't, you wouldn't be my student."

"Would it matter if I wasn't in your class? I'd still be a student, and you'd still be a professor at the school I attend. It has to be against the rules, right?"

Jacob nodded. "I'm kind of afraid to find out."

"What do you mean?"

"I don't want to know. I've avoided looking it up or asking Luke about it. I guess I don't want some stupid rule telling me I can't be with you. I *want* to be oblivious."

"I don't understand," Avery said.

"I'm not making any sense." He grabbed her hands again, his emerald green eyes locked on hers. His thumb rubbed circles on her knuckles. "Let me put this as plainly as possible: I want to be with you, Avery. I want to give this relationship a shot. Despite the rules, despite everything. We can make this work. It won't be easy, though. You're the one who needs to decide what you want. If you don't want a relationship with me, then I'll settle for being your teacher, and hopefully, your friend. Your choice."

Avery's heart skipped a beat. She wanted more too. She was out of her mind—certifiably insane—but she wanted it. Wanted him.

"I want it as much as you do."

A grin spread across Jacob's face. "Yeah?"

"Yes," Avery replied. She picked up an onion ring and shoved it in her mouth. "This is going to be difficult, isn't it?"

"Yes." Jacob leaned over the table. "And complicated. Are you okay with that?"

Avery's heart thumped out of control. Jacob ignited something in her. When she was with him, she felt alive, beautiful, and wanted. She wasn't ready or willing to walk away from that. She dragged in a deep breath before she spoke.

"It's going to be hard, and sometimes I won't like it. I doubt you will too. We'll have to figure it out as we go along. But I think we can make it work, even if we have to keep it a secret. Let's give it a chance."

Jacob's smile lit up his face. He had gorgeous crinkles at the corner of his eyes and the green sparkled like dewy grass hit by morning sunlight. "Come here," he said.

Avery moved to the other side of the table and slid into the seat beside him. Jacob slipped his arm around her waist and tugged her against his side. He kissed her, his lips soft and sweet.

She sighed and snuggled closer to her professor. All complications disappeared when she was in his arms. She didn't think about anything else, only Jacob.

Chapter 7

Jacob

"Spill it, dude," Luke demanded. "You've been in a good mood for the last few weeks, and I want to know what the hell is going on." He took a sip of his cold beer and stared at his best friend, a smile playing around his lips.

"I don't know what you're talking about," Jacob said.

There was no way he was going to let Luke in on his secret. Everything was too new; he and Avery were still in the discovery stage. It had only been a couple of weeks since they had agreed to give their relationship a shot—rules be damned—and he had no intention of ruining it by opening his big mouth. He fiddled with his beer bottle, picking at the label, and refused to meet Luke's eyes.

"You're a shitty liar," Luke muttered, shaking his head. "I haven't seen you in this good of a mood in a long time. Since before Rome. Not since you and Maggie got—" His mouth snapped shut. "Sorry," he mumbled.

"I can talk about it. It won't break me." Jacob laughed. "It's been five years."

"You haven't mentioned it since you moved back to the states. You never explained what happened. One day everything was fine, and the next, you were packing your stuff and moving to Italy."

Jacob downed his bottle of beer and signaled their server, Trista, for another one. She set it in front of him, smiled shyly at Luke, then scurried away.

"Somebody has a crush." He snorted, nodding in Trista's direction.

Luke pointed at the center of his chest. "Engaged, remember? And you're changing the subject."

"There wasn't anything to explain," he said. "It was over between me and Maggie. End of story."

"I repeat, you're a shitty liar." His friend smiled and bumped his shoulder into Jacob's. "Tell me what happened."

Jacob exhaled, his fingers tapping on the bar top. "We were engaged."

Luke sputtered, beer flying from his mouth in a cascade of amber droplets. "You were what?"

He couldn't help but laugh; he'd never heard Luke screech. Sobering, Jacob scrubbed a hand over his bearded face and sighed. "I asked Maggie to marry me, and she said yes. We were engaged for almost a year."

Luke let out a low whistle. "How the hell did you keep it a secret?"

"We agreed to keep it quiet. Her parents wouldn't approve, not while we were both in school. We figured when we graduated, we'd get married."

"Jesus, Jake, that's crazy. What happened?"

He took a drink and wiped his lips with the back of his hand. "We fought all the time. About everything. She wanted to stay in Lakeside, settle down in our hometown, and make a life for ourselves. It wasn't what I wanted. Then I got the job in Rome."

"And you left."

"I left. I broke off the engagement, packed my shit, and took the job in Italy. I didn't think I'd ever come back here or see Maggie again."

Luke shook his head and chuckled. "Holy shit. She's probably pissed at you."

Jacob rolled his eyes. "Gee, thanks, Luke, I never thought of that. I can always count on you to make me feel better."

"Sorry." Luke grinned. "Have you talked to Maggie?"

Jacob nodded. "Yes."

"Shit, how did it go?"

"Okay, I guess." Jacob shrugged. "She wants something. I just don't know what."

"Maybe she wants to get back together?" Luke suggested.

Jacob shook his head hard enough to hurt his neck. "Oh no, not going down that road again."

"Are you interested in dating at all?" Luke asked. "Or are you putting your love life on the shelf?"

"You don't give up, do you?" Jacob chuckled. He downed the rest of his beer, set the bottle on the bar, and rose to his feet. "Right now, the only thing I'm interested in is settling into my job and my new place. The rest will come later."

Luke narrowed his eyes and shook his head. "I'm convinced there is a woman. You're too damn happy. But I'll drop it for now. You'll tell me when you're ready."

Jacob shrugged and clapped Luke on the shoulder. "Not likely," he joked. He pulled his wallet free and dropped some cash to the table. "I gotta go."

"It's early," Luke protested.

"I've got things to do." Avery was due at his place in a couple of hours. He still had to pick up dinner and straighten up before she got there.

"Uh, huh." His best friend shook his head. "There's something you're not telling me. I'm your best friend, asshole. You can trust me. Tell me what the hell has you so happy."

Jacob laughed. "Life, Luke. Life is good right now."

—

Avery perched on the edge of her chair, wine glass in hand, her brown eyes dark with worry. She'd been unusually quiet all night.

"You okay?" Jacob asked.

"I'm tired, I guess."

He kneeled beside her, took her chin between his fingers, and forced her to look at him. "We're already lying to the outside world, Avery. Let's not lie to each other. Something is wrong. Tell me what it is."

"You mean, aside from the fact we *are* lying to everyone? Which is a fabulous way to start a relationship." She took a sip of her wine with a shaking hand.

Jacob rested his hand on her waist and squeezed. "Is that what it is? The lying and secrecy?"

"Yes." She finished the wine in her glass and reached for the bottle, glass clinking together as she poured. "I want this to work. There's something about you, Jacob, something I can't put into words. There's a connection between us—"

He nodded. It was an indescribable connection. It pleased him that she felt it as well.

"Nat asked me where I was going when I left the apartment, and I couldn't tell her. On the way here, all I could think about was how happy I am, yet I can't tell anyone." Avery pushed a hand through her hair. "The secret keeping, it's just, well, it's hard to deal with. I can't tell anyone about us even though I want to scream it from the top of the Psych building. It...well, it makes me feel like I'm not good enough."

Jacob rubbed circles on her back, a poor attempt to soothe her. Guilt weighed heavily on his heart. He was the reason they had to keep their relationship a secret. It wasn't fair. To either of them.

"I'm sorry." He sighed. "You are perfect. You deserve the world, sweetheart, not someone who keeps you a secret."

Avery gave him a grim smile. "I want this, Jake. I want you. God, I'm sorry. I'm ruining our date with all my doom and gloom." She kissed him, her lips lingering on his. "Forgive me?"

"There's nothing to forgive." Their lips brushed as he spoke. "Let's eat."

After they finished dinner, they moved to the living room with the wine. Jacob put a movie on, but instead of watching it, they talked with the television playing quietly in the background. It was a good start to filling in the gaps left by the early whirlwind of their relationship.

It was almost midnight when Avery pushed herself to her feet with a sigh and grabbed her shoes.

"I should go," she said.

Jacob walked her to the door, wrapped her in his arms, and kissed her. She clung to his neck, her face upturned, body flush against his. He held her close, not wanting to let her go. With one last kiss, she left.

Not tired, he decided to clean the kitchen. He opened a beer and put the leftover food in the fridge, staring out the window into the backyard as he waited for the sink to fill with water. He was so caught up in the thoughts running through his head, it took him a minute to realize someone was tapping on the back door. He dried off his hands and tossed the towel on the table before he opened the door.

Avery stood there, shifting from foot to foot, her lower lip caught between her teeth.

"Avery? Is everything okay?"

She didn't say a word. She stepped inside, dropped her bag to the floor, slid her arms around his waist, and kissed him.

Chapter 8

Avery

"I don't want to leave," Avery whispered.

The air was thick and tense, electric heat thrumming between them. Avery dragged in a shaky breath but was cut off by Jacob's mouth crashing into hers, kissing her long and hard. She pushed up into the kiss, her breasts pressed to his chest. A low moan escaped her. It had been too long since anyone kissed her the way Jacob kissed did—tender and sweet, with an underlying current of desperation and need. Her body burned with desire.

Jacob's hands slid down her sides and over her ass. He lifted Avery and set her on the counter, stepped between her open legs, and pulled her forward. His hips nestled against hers, his arousal hard behind the thick denim of his jeans. Avery's head fell back as he kissed her jaw, her neck, her mouth. Every touch of his lips made her ache for more.

She moaned and wrapped her legs around Jacob's thighs, her hand tangling in his hair, holding him close as the kiss deepened. Avery fumbled with the button on his jeans impatiently and tugged them open.

Jacob stepped back, his full, pink lips kiss-swollen, the pupils of his green eyes blown wide with lust. His chest heaved and his full cock strained for release behind his partially undone pants. His hands clenched into fists at his side.

"Jesus Christ, Avery, let me catch my breath," he panted. "Are you sure about this?"

Avery's stomach dropped and bile rose in her throat. If he turned her away, she wouldn't be able to handle it. She'd sat in her car for five minutes debating with herself, weighing the pros and cons of having sex with her professor. Despite the multitude of reasons not to take that step, she circled back to her inexplicable and desperate need for the professor. Screw the problems that might arise; she wanted Professor Jacob Moore more than she'd ever wanted anyone, and she would risk it all for him.

"Yes," she replied. "Aren't you?"

Jacob pounced and pressed his mouth on hers. The all-consuming kiss was the only answer she needed.

"I guess that's a yes," she giggled when he released her.

"It's a hell yes," Jacob growled. His arm slid around her and he pushed back between her legs, holding her on the counter with his body. His breath was warm against her skin. "Do you know how much I want you?"

Avery opened her mouth to speak; nothing came out but a weak squeak. She swallowed and tried again.

"Show me."

He kissed her, taking her breath away and making her heart race. She clung to Jacob as if she were drowning and he was her life preserver. It left no doubt in her mind about how much he wanted her.

Jacob yanked her t-shirt off and dropped it to the floor, moaning low in the back of his throat as he wrapped his lips around her lace covered breast and sucked. He kneaded the other breast, his thumb circling the nipple, flicking the hardening nub.

Heat pooled deep in the pit of her stomach, and a fine sheen of sweat broke out over her body. She hooked her leg around his ass and pulled him closer, writhing against him, desperate for some friction.

Jacob's lips moved up her neck and across her jaw. He intertwined his fingers with hers as he nibbled on her ear-lobe and pulled her hand between their bodies. "I need you to touch me, baby," he said. "Please."

Avery slipped her hand under his boxers and down the length of his shaft. Her hand wrapped around his cock, and a shaky groan left him. His hips moved with her hand, his kisses increasing in intensity as she caressed him. Jacob's hands moved all over her body, tugging at her clothes until she sat on his kitchen counter in nothing but panties. He buried his face between her breasts, kissing, licking, and nipping at her skin as his hands slid up her thighs, moving closer to where she needed them.

He dragged his fingers up her leg, skimmed the edge of her panties, and slipped a finger beneath them to caress her damp folds. She moaned and squirmed as her head fell back. Her hips rose off the counter as two of Jacob's fingers eased into her, caressing her until she saw stars and gasped his name. He didn't stop and dragged her to the edge of the counter, two fingers deep, the palm of his hand pressed against her. His mouth swallowed her obscene groans as she came on his fingers, her slick running over his hand.

Jacob released her long enough to kick off his shoes and remove his clothes. Then he eased a condom down his length and was back on her in an instant, sliding her wet panties down and tossing them aside before he entered her. He peppered her neck and shoulders with kisses as he slowly pumped his hips, giving her time to adjust to his substantial size. The hands on her ass yanked her closer with every thrust, so tight and perfect she wasn't sure how long she could take it. It was almost too much—a pleasure so insanely wonderful it bordered on painful.

"Lean back," he ordered.

Avery did as she was told and leaned back on her hands, heat rising in her cheeks as Jacob stared at her, devouring her with his eyes as his hands ran over every inch and curve of her body. He praised her—sweet words that made her head spin and her heart pound.

Jacob's fingers dug into her ass as he slammed into her, his cock dragging against her sweet spot every time he pulled out and his taut abs brushing her clit with each thrust.

Avery was on the edge, so close it wouldn't take much to push her over. She locked eyes with Jacob and slid her hand down her stomach and between her legs. She circled her clit with two fingers while Jacob pounded into her, his eyes blown wide. His cock twitched and pulsed as she climaxed, her orgasm exploding through her.

Jacob groaned and thrust harder, burying himself inside her, his tight, hard thrusts prolonging her pleasure, dragging it out until she was dizzy with the sensations overwhelming her. He came with a quiet grunt against her lips.

He held her, his lips gently caressing her neck and shoulder. He slid her off the counter, set her on her feet, and disposed of the condom. Avery held onto the counter, her head still spinning from the incredible sex.

Jacob held his hand out to her, a smirk on his face. She took it and returned his smile.

"Come on, let's go to the bedroom."

"Bedroom?" she repeated.

"Well, yeah," he chuckled. "I'm not done with you yet." He wrapped his arm around her waist and tugged her tight against his side. "If that's okay with you?"

Avery giggled and pressed a lingering kiss to his lips.

"I'll take that as a yes," he echoed her words back at her and winked, then he led her up the stairs to his bedroom.

Chapter 9

Avery

*T*he shower turned off as Avery slipped her shirt over her head. Jacob walked out of the bathroom a few minutes later with a towel around his waist, his hair still wet and dripping down his broad shoulders and his taut chest. It should be illegal for one man to be so attractive.

"Hey, are you leaving?" he asked. He kept one hand on the towel, holding it in place as he rifled through the top drawer of his dresser. Boxer briefs in hand, he slammed the drawer shut with his elbow.

"Yeah. I have class in a couple hours." She tied her shoes and stood up, her eyes darting around the room, trying to remember where she'd left her purse. Her brain wasn't firing on all cylinders; the only thing she'd been able to think about was Jacob and all the things she wanted him to do to her. "Have you seen my purse?"

"I think it's downstairs in the living room. Or maybe the office." He leaned in for a kiss. "Or the kitchen or the hallway—"

"Is this where my purse might be or a replay of all the places we had sex last night?" She giggled.

Jacob chuckled and shrugged, an adorable smile on his face. Avery returned the smile and kiss, resisting the urge to yank off the towel and push Jacob down on the bed. She needed to get back and shower before her first class. She forced herself to break off the kiss and stepped away, patting his cheek.

"Hurry and get dressed so you can tell me goodbye," she said as she walked out of Jacob's bedroom. Downstairs, she found her purse on the couch, put on her jacket, pulled an orange juice from the fridge, and leaned against the kitchen counter. In less than five minutes, Jacob stood in front of her. She stepped into the hug he offered and rested her head on his shoulder.

"Are you okay?" He pushed her hair off her neck and kissed her throat.

"No, not really." Avery sighed. "I hate this."

"I'm sorry," he whispered against her neck.

"I know," she mumbled.

Jacob was always sorry; it seemed to be the only thing he'd said over the last few weeks since the first time they had sex. He was sorry he couldn't take her on a real date, sorry she had to sneak in and out of his house through the back door, sorry he couldn't call her, sorry they couldn't walk into class together as a couple, sorry, sorry, sorry, sorry. She'd heard him apologize more in the last three weeks than she'd heard anyone apologize in her entire life.

"Most of the time, I'm okay with how things are," Avery said.

Jacob rested his chin on top of her head and hugged her close. "Most of the time?"

"Yes, most of the time. Do I wish we could have a normal relationship and not hide it from everyone? Of course, I do. But I know it's not possible right now. I can wait. At least I think I can. I'll take what we've got for now. But I get angry and frustrated with the university's archaic rules forcing us to hide our relationship sometimes. If Professor Hess were here, he would be my professor, not you, and all of this wouldn't matter. We would be freely together."

"I'll make it up to you, sweetheart. I swear. As soon as I can."

"I know you will." She pulled him into a deep kiss. "I have to go. I'll talk to you later." She stepped out of his embrace, snatched her purse off the counter, and slipped out the back door. She could feel Jacob's eyes on her as she hurried across the lawn and out the side gate.

She'd parked her car a couple of blocks over next to a little neighborhood playground. Caught up in her thoughts, she stepped off the curb blindly. A black motorcycle sped down the street in front of her, and a startled squeak left her as she stumbled back to avoid getting hit. Avery cursed under her breath and pulled her coat tight around herself, shivering in the chilly morning air. She rushed to get in the car, turned on the heat right away, and checked the clock. She had less than two hours before her first class.

"Shit, shit, shit," she grumbled, checking her mirror before pulling into traffic. She'd be lucky if she made it on time.

———

Avery wasn't on time, and it threw her entire day off. She had to take a cold shower because Nat used all the hot water. Then she forgot to grab her English literature paper off the printer and had to skip lunch to detour to the library to print another copy. By the time she slid into her seat in Professor Moore's class, ten minutes late, she was in a terrible mood—tired, hungry, irritable, and her head felt like it might explode. She wanted to go home and take a nap. Jacob's disapproving look certainly didn't make her feel any better.

Doing her best to ignore Professor Moore and not make eye contact, she pulled her laptop from her bag, powered it up, and copied the notes from the board while she listened to the lecture. The headache pounded in the center of her forehead, and it only got worse by the minute. It was impossible to concentrate.

Her phone lit up with an incoming message. She slid her finger across the screen to find a message from Carson, her friend and co-worker.

[Carson: Come out with us tonight. We miss you.]

Avery smiled. She hadn't gone out with her friends in weeks, not since she started seeing Jacob. She typed a reply.

[Avery: Who's us?]

[Carson: Me, Brick, Nat. We're going to Time Out to shoot pool and drink beer.]

[Avery: I'm not sure I should. I've had a bad day. I'm tired, hungry, and I'm getting a headache. I wouldn't be much fun.]

[Carson: I have the perfect remedy for that. Come hang out with your friends. It will be fun. We miss you.]

Carson was right. Maybe she needed a night out to do something normal. Jacob would understand.

[Avery: Okay. But you have to feed me before we drink, otherwise, I'll be a mess.]

[Carson: Deal! Meet us at Time Out at 7.]

Avery scrubbed a hand over her face and sighed. The secrets were starting to have a toll despite her best efforts. Hiding her relationship with Jacob was getting harder, especially as her feelings for the professor grew. And though she told Jacob she would take whatever she could get from him, she couldn't help but long for a normal relationship—one where they could go on a real date, one where she didn't have to sneak in and out of his house, one where they could walk around town as a couple.

"Ms. Collins, may I speak to you for a moment?" Jacob interrupted her musings, drawing her attention back to the front of the class.

She jumped; she hadn't realized class was over. Avery cleared her throat and rose to her feet. "Of course, Professor Moore."

She shoved her things in her bag and pushed past the other students leaving the room, making her way past them down the stairs. Another student stood in front of the professor with her arms crossed and a hip jutting out, smacking her gum.

Jacob leaned against his desk, arms crossed over his chest in mirror, nodding at the young lady standing in front of him. He glanced at Avery and held up one finger.

"Three days, Ms. Small," he stated. "You can miss three days a semester. I made that clear in the syllabus."

The young woman—Avery thought her name was Becky—huffed and rolled her eyes. "I hoped you would make an exception for me." She took a step closer to Jacob and smiled up at him. "Just this once?"

Professor Moore shook his head. "I don't make exceptions. You can audit the class for no credit, or you can drop it and take it next semester."

"Fine," Becky huffed. She spun on her heel, her elbow smacking Avery as she pushed past her and stomped up the stairs.

"Wow," Avery mouthed.

Jacob straightened, towering over her. "Hey, you okay?" he asked, keeping his voice low. The door closed behind Becky, and he stepped closer to Avery, ducked his head, and pressed a kiss to the corner of her mouth.

Tears pooled in the corner of her eyes. She swallowed past the lump rising in her throat. She shrugged. "I'm having a crappy day. Whatever could go wrong, did."

"Oh, babe, I'm sorry," Jacob whispered. "Is there anything I can do?"

She shook her head. "No. You know what? I'm gonna go out with my friends tonight. I need...I need to do something normal, you know? Not hide out at your house for the night."

A pained expression crossed Jacob's face, gone so quickly she wondered if she'd really seen it. He nodded and kissed the top of her head. "Of course." He pushed a hand through his hair and chuckled. "Funny you should bring that up. Luke's been harassing me to go out with him for a beer. It might do us both good to have a night out."

Avery nodded and pushed up on her toes to kiss him. "I'll call you later, okay?"

"Have fun!" he called as she sprinted up the stairs.

———

Avery slumped in the booth and sipped her margarita, watching Carson and Brick play darts. She couldn't get the image of Jacob and his pained expression and the feeling she had upset him out of her head. It shouldn't bother her, but it did. She took her phone from her pocket, hoping he texted. He hadn't, so she sent him one, attempting to smooth things over.
[Avery: Having fun, miss you tho!]

So what if it was a lie? Half of it anyway; she missed him, but she wasn't having fun. He didn't need to know that. She shoved her phone into her back pocket. Nat appeared at the table with more drinks, french fries, and nachos in her hand. She set everything down and dropped into the seat across from Avery, a perfectly shaped red eyebrow raised and her head tipped to one side.

"Are you okay?" Nat asked.

"People keep asking me that, and it's getting old," Avery grumbled, shoving a fry into her mouth. "I'm fine."

"Okay, sheesh, grumpy, sorry," Nat said, hands up and a smirk on her face. "What? Are you tired from the late night you had?"

"What?" Avery feigned innocence.

Her friend rolled her eyes. "Please. When are you gonna tell me who he is?"

"What do you mean?"

"I know you're seeing someone, Avery. You're spending a lot of nights away from home, you act all secretive, and you hide in your room to talk on the phone. Are you going to tell me who it is or not?"

She shrugged. "I'll tell you when I'm ready. And I'm not ready." Except she was. She desperately wanted to tell someone, wanted someone to know how happy she was, how good Jacob made her feel, and how she might be falling in love with Professor Moore.

"Oh my God, is that Professor Moore?"

Avery's head snapped up. It was as if thinking about him had somehow summoned him to the bar. "What? Where?" She turned around, looking in the direction Nat pointed.

"Over there, on the other side of the bar."

Jacob was standing on the other side of the room with a couple of other professors, Luke Campbell and Margaret Hudspeth from the Science department, along with a brunette she didn't recognize. Avery turned back around before he saw her, ducking behind the high-backed booth.

Jealousy twisted through the pit of her stomach, and she had to resist the urge to throw herself out of the booth, stalk across the room, and slap Professor Hudspeth across her pretty face. Instead, she grabbed her drink and downed it in a few swallows. She wiped a hand across her mouth, grimacing as her head spun from the onslaught of alcohol.

"Are you okay?" The surprise on Nat's face would have been funny if Avery wasn't so pissed.

"I'm gonna need more margaritas," she muttered.

Chapter 10

Jacob

Jacob stopped inside the door and looked around, trying to find Luke in the crowd of people. Friday night at Time Out was busier than he expected. College students filled the place, along with a few townspeople he recognized and staff from the university. This was the place to be on the weekend.

"Jake!"

Luke waved at him from the other side of the bar; luckily, he towered over everyone at 6'5" and was easy to spot in a crowd. Jacob weaved through the crowd, elbowing people out of the way until he reached his friend.

Luke clapped him on the back and shoved a beer into his hand. "Don't be mad," he muttered.

Jacob narrowed his eyes and glared at him. "Why would I be mad?"

Luke didn't have time to answer because Luke's fiancée, Bonnie, appeared at Luke's side. "Jacob! You made it!" She pressed a kiss to his cheek and squeezed his arm. "Look who I brought!"

Maggie stood behind Bonnie, smirking. "Hello, Jacob."

"Maggie. Long time no see." He brought his bottle of beer to his mouth and downed it.

Maggie snorted, pushed past him to lean over the bar, and ordered a drink. She turned around and rested her elbows on the bar behind her, eyes narrowed, bright red lips pursed in irritation. She surveyed the room.

"Why are we here again? This place is filled with students." She said "students" as if the word left an unpleasant taste in her mouth. "Why don't we go to Ronnie's?"

"It's closed." Bonnie shrugged. "It's only open from June through August. The only other bar in town is the Elks' Lodge."

Maggie rolled her eyes and shook her head. She turned back to the bar, picked up her drink, and slipped onto a barstool, her head propped on her hand. She patted the seat next to her.

"Come here, Jacob. Sit down and keep an old friend company."

He ignored her, propping himself at the end of the bar and watched the crowd. Luke and Bonnie excused themselves to grab a pool table, leaving him alone with Maggie.

Maggie slid onto the seat beside him. She put her hand on his arm and bumped her shoulder into his. "Can't we try to get along? For the sake of our friends?"

"I wasn't expecting you to be here. I'm not trying to be difficult. I swear. But I don't want you—or anyone else—to get the wrong idea."

Maggie blanched, irritation crossing her face, but she quickly recovered. She cleared her throat. "I don't think anyone will get the wrong idea. We're just friends, Jacob. Nothing more. We can spend an occasional evening together without people thinking we're in love."

"We have a history, Mags—"

"One that no one knows about except Luke. We're adults, and we should act like it."

Maybe Maggie was right. Their relationship was in the past. Way in the past. It was time for them to move on. If she could act like an adult, so could he. All he wanted was an evening out with his friends and a chance to take his mind off his growing problems with Avery and their relationship. If he let this shit with Maggie bother him, it would only compound those problems.

Luke waved at him from the pool tables. He nodded, grabbed his beer, and said to Maggie, "I think they got a pool table. Come on. Let's see if I can still kick your ass."

Maggie raised an eyebrow but smiled before she hopped off the barstool and followed him to the pool tables.

The evening turned out better than he expected. Once he got past the frustration of Maggie had intruding on the night, he enjoyed himself. He and Luke played game after game of pool, getting more competitive as the evening wore on. Jacob nursed his way through two beers, intent on keeping his head on straight. It didn't stop him from having fun.

He tried to ignore Maggie flirting with him. Not that it was easy when she laid it on so thick—touching his arm, laughing too long at his stupid jokes, leaning against the table beside him, her expensive floral scent thick in the air. Everything was fine until Bonnie decided they should play two-on-two, teaming him up with Maggie. The flirting only intensified.

"Come help me line this shot up, handsome," Maggie teased, pointing at the pool table. "If I miss it, we lose."

Jacob exhaled, but rather than start an argument, or worse, suffer the wrath of an irritated Maggie, he leaned over her, positioned her hands on the pool cue, and helped her line up the shot. The shot cued up, he backed away, grabbed his beer, and moved to the end of the table. Ignoring Mags and her flirting was tiresome; he was ready to call it a night. After this game, he was going home.

Luke went next, then it was Jacob's turn. He took a swig of his beer, grabbed his pool cue, and turned toward the table. A pair of familiar brown eyes locked with his.

Avery stood near the bar, her face almost green. Without thinking, he took a step toward her, but she shook her head and turned away. He watched her wobble across the room, obviously drunk.

Jacob tried to concentrate on the game of pool, but he kept finding himself looking for Avery in the crowd, worried about her. After a few minutes, he watched her head for the front door. He took his last shot, propped his pool cue against the wall, and set his beer bottle down.

"I'll be right back," he said, pulling his jacket on.

He made his way through the crowd, ignoring Maggie and Luke calling after him as he followed Avery out the door. Consequences be damned, there was no way he would let her go home alone, not when she looked too drunk to make any wise decisions.

I need to take care of Avery.

Chapter 11

Avery

*A*very did her best to ignore Jacob on the other side of the room, laughing and having a good time. But as the night wore on, she constantly looked over her shoulder, watching him. Bitter envy roared through her veins whenever Professor Hudspeth touched Jacob; the sight made her stomach roll. Every time Hudspeth brushed up against her professor, Avery reached for her drink, hoping it would help ease the pain and obliterate the jealousy. When Jacob leaned over her to help Professor Hudspeth line up a shot, Avery shoved herself out of the booth, stumbling over Nat's feet as she excused herself and hurried through the crowd to the restroom.

She stepped into the first empty stall, slammed it shut, and threw the lock just before her gorge rose and everything she ingested came flying out. Muffled "ews" and the sound of shuffling feet filled the room, then silence. She prayed the bathroom had emptied so she could puke in private, something she hadn't done since her freshman year of college.

Avery braced a hand on the stall door and pushed herself to her feet, grimacing at the filthy bathroom floor she kneeled on. She made her way to the sink, stopping every few feet when a wave of dizziness washed over her. She rinsed out her mouth, splashed water on her face, then left the bathroom.

Halfway across the massive room, she stopped and leaned against the end of the bar, her head spinning and her stomach clenching uncomfortably. Jacob stood beside one of the pool tables, his beer held between two fingers, a smile teasing the corners of his mouth. When he turned to line up his shot, his eyes landed on Avery. He straightened, concern coloring his features. He took a step toward her, but she shook her head, turned, and pushed her way through the mass of people.

Avery eased into the booth beside Carson and forced a weak smile onto her face. It was time to go. So much for a night out with her friends. She snatched an unopened bottle of water from the middle of the table and took a sip. She patted Carson on the arm.

"Give me my purse, would you, Car? I'm gonna go."

Before he could give it to her, Nat grabbed it and dumped it out on the table. She dug Avery's keys out of the pile, took her car key off the ring, shoved everything back inside, and set it in front of her.

"You're not driving," Nat said. "You've had too much to drink."

"Fine, whatever," Avery grumbled. She slid out of the booth, her purse clutched in one hand and phone in the other. "I'll call an Uber or Lyft."

She threw herself out of the booth and stomped out of the bar, ignoring her friends shouting after her, desperate to get away from them, from Jacob, from everyone.

Outside, she passed the window and saw Jacob and Professor Hudspeth. The gorgeous professor had a hip propped against the table and her arms crossed over her substantial chest, her perfect, blood-red lips pursed in what could only be irritation. Avery leaned against the wall beside the window, intent on staying there no longer than a minute or two to catch her breath. When she tried to push away, a wave of dizziness hit her.

"Damn it." She fell back against the wall, her cell phone falling to the ground. "Shit." She closed her eyes and concentrated on not throwing up again.

"Here."

Jacob stood in front of her, her cell phone in his hand. She took it from him and shoved it in her back pocket.

"What are you doing out here?" she asked.

"Hello to you, too." He put his hand on her arm, stroking it. "You don't look so good, sweetheart."

"I don't feel so good," she muttered. "I've had too much to drink, and I was trying to get an Uber..."

The door opened behind Jacob, and Professor Hudspeth peered around the corner. "Hey, it's your turn."

"Hey, Maggie." Jacob shifted on his feet. "This is Avery. She's one of my students."

"Hello," Professor Hudspeth—Maggie—said, her eyes flicking Avery's way before turning back to Jacob. "Are you coming? It's your turn."

"I think I'm going to drive Avery home," he told her. "Could you tell Luke and Bonnie goodbye for me?"

Maggie stepped outside, a confused look on her face. "Um, are you sure, Jacob?"

He nodded and took hold of Avery's elbow. "It's fine. Trust me, Mags, okay?"

Maggie grimaced, her chin tipping in a brief nod. "I'll talk to you later." It sounded more like a demand than a promise.

Jacob grunted and steered Avery away from the bar toward his car. He opened the passenger door, helped her inside, then jogged around the front and climbed in.

Avery snorted. "Are you sure you don't want to stay here with Maggie? I can still get a ride."

"No, I don't want to stay here with Maggie. I've never seen you like this. What is wrong with you?"

"It's called jealousy, Professor Moore," she snapped. She pressed her fingers to the center of her forehead and rubbed. "It's what happens when you spend the evening watching some woman fawn all over your boyfriend. Wait, I'm sorry, I'm not supposed to call you that, am I? You're not my boyfriend. You're the professor I'm secretly screwing." She hated herself even as the words came out of her mouth.

Out of the corner of her eye, she saw Jacob's mouth open then snap shut. He gnawed at his lower lip, his brow furrowed. His knuckles were white on the steering wheel. He exhaled loudly.

"That's not fair, Avery."

She sighed. "Nothing about this is fair. Fair would have been meeting you after I graduated, or you not being a professor at the university I attend. Fair would have been anything other than this. Sometimes it's too much to deal with, and today was one of those days." She scrubbed a hand over her face and looked out the window. "Where are we going?"

"Your apartment."

"We're not going back to your place?" She assumed when he'd offered to take her home, he meant his home. She was wrong.

"No," Jacob said. "You need to sleep off the alcohol. I think it's best if you go home."

Tears pricked the corners of her eyes, and her heart stuttered in her chest. She leaned her head against the frosty glass and closed her eyes, the soothing jazz music on the radio lulling her into a state of semi-consciousness. It was quiet until Jacob stopped in front of her apartment building.

"Drink a bottle of water and take a couple of aspirin," he said and leaned over her to push open the passenger door, his scent making her head spin. He didn't make eye contact.

Avery dragged herself wordlessly from the car, the heavy door creaking as she closed it. Jacob pulled back onto the street without so much as a glance back.

Her heart hurt as she watched him drive away. She dug her house key out of her purse, swung around, and tried to unlock the door, her shaking hands making it damn near impossible. A loud noise echoed off the wall. She squeaked and spun around so quickly she lost her balance and stumbled back against the door. A black motorcycle flew by, heading in the same direction as Jacob.

"Jesus Christ," she mumbled. "Asshole."

Another tenant came out of the building and pushed past her, so she grabbed the edge of the door and slipped inside. She raced up the stairs, her stomach churning, and frantically unlocked the apartment door, praying she wouldn't puke in the hallway. She ran through the apartment and fell to her knees in front of the toilet right before she threw up.

Avery fell asleep—passed out—and woke up shortly after curled in the fetal position on the bathroom floor, a wadded towel under her head. Her body ached, and her head throbbed. Sitting up caused another wave of nausea to wash over her. She waited for it to pass before pushing to her feet, mumbling curses under her breath when the room spun.

Avery dug through the medicine cabinet over the sink, grabbed the bottle of pain meds, and made her way to the kitchen. She swallowed two of the tiny white pills with some water, grimacing as they slid down her raw throat. The nausea crept back as she shucked off her clothes, fading only once she dropped to the bed and pulled the pillow over her head. She prayed Nat would stay at Brick's so she could get some sleep. The last thing she needed was her nosy roommate interrupting her sleep to interrogate her. If the look on Nat's face when Avery left the bar was any indication, that was exactly what she planned to do.

Avery fell into a restless sleep plagued with dreams of chasing Professor Moore through a dark forest, repeatedly losing him to a giant, red dragon.

—

She woke with the taste of stale beer and regret on her tongue. The room spun, and her head pounded. She dragged in a deep breath and blew it out.

I am never drinking again.

Avery grabbed her phone from the end table where she dropped it and slid her finger across the screen. There were no messages from Jacob, though there were a couple from her friends—Nat telling her she stayed over at Brick's and Carson checking on her. Her finger hovered over Jacob's name in her contacts for a second. Instead of calling him, Avery crawled out of bed to the bathroom. Forty-five minutes later, she'd showered, brushed her teeth, and had some toast and coffee.

It wasn't until she dug through her purse to find her car key that she remembered her car was at the bar and Nat had her key. It took her twenty minutes to find the spare key in a box under her bed. Then Avery ordered an Uber.

Twenty minutes later, she stepped out of the rideshare vehicle in the Time Out parking lot beside her car. She thanked the driver—a sweet, older lady who chatted about her favorite TV shows during the drive—one last time before she pulled the key from her purse and watched the car drive away. She brushed the snow from the windshield. The weather had taken a turn overnight, a storm moving in from Canada leaving a thick layer of snow over everything and bringing a bitter, chilly wind. Her fingers were numb by the time she climbed inside; she'd left her gloves on the kitchen counter.

She sent up a silent prayer the car would start and turned the key. To her surprise, it did on the first try. Avery waited for it to warm up while her head and heart waged a fierce argument over what she should do. After a few minutes, she pushed a hand through her hair, gripped the steering wheel tight, and pulled out of the parking lot.

Avery knew where she had to go and what she had to do.

Chapter 12

Jacob

He went straight home after dropping Avery at her apartment, replaying their conversation—and his actions—in his head as he drove. Once he was home, he didn't bother to turn on any lights; he went straight to his room, peeled off his clothes, and fell into bed. Jacob's limbs were heavy, his throat thick, and his eyes dry. He was asleep seconds after his head hit the pillow.

The incessant tapping woke him, along with the sun shining through his bedroom window and his neighbor's barking dog. He sat up and checked the clock. It was after ten. No wonder he was disoriented; he hadn't slept this late since college.

The tapping continued. He pushed himself out of bed, yanked on his jeans and a t-shirt, and followed the sound to his back door. He yanked it open and a sharp wind hit him smack in the face, taking his breath away. Or maybe it was the woman standing at his door.

"Avery?" he mumbled. "What are you doing here? I was going to call you when I woke up." He pushed a hand through his sleep-tousled hair.

Avery smiled and shrugged one shoulder. Wisps of her blonde hair escaped her emerald hat, and her curves disappeared underneath her large, puffy jacket. She gnawed on her lower lip for a second before responding.

"I-I wanted to apologize."

Jacob shook his head before she finished speaking, grabbed her hand, and yanked her inside. The door slammed closed behind her. "No. You have nothing to apologize for. I would have reacted the same way if I had to watch someone—ex or not—putting their hands all over you. I'm the one who should apologize. I'm sorry you had to see that."

Tears glistened in Avery's eyes as she nodded. She smiled, but it didn't reach her eyes.

Jacob took her chin and forced her to look at him. "Avery, baby, there's something I need you to understand. *You* are the only woman I want. I have no feelings for Maggie. None. She is my past. You are my present."

Avery threw her arms around Jacob's neck, her body flush against his, and pressed a trembling kiss to his lips.

Jacob's mouth slanted over hers, his thumbs caressing the soft skin of her cheeks. He released her to drag her deeper into the house, down the hall, and into the living room. She dropped her heavy coat and hat on the couch, gasping in surprise when Jacob pushed her against the wall, impatient to get his hands on her. He slid his hand beneath her heavy sweater and up her side to cup her breast as he pushed his knee between her legs. He twisted his fingers in her hair and tipped her head back, his lips roaming over her neck.

"Mm, Professor Moore," Avery moaned.

"Fuck, Avery," he snarled and ripped open the front of her jeans. His hand slipped into her underwear and caressed her until she ground against his exploring fingers. He eased his middle finger into her, his thumb circling her clit.

"Touch me, sweetheart."

Avery unbuttoned his jeans and took him in her hand, stroking him, drawing a thick moan from him. He shoved her jeans and underwear down her legs. She pulled away from him, kicked off her shoes and pants, then yanked the sweater over her head, tossing it on the floor.

He wanted her, needed her. He couldn't wait a second longer. Jacob pounced. He pushed his jeans down to free his throbbing length, groaning when the sensitive tip brushed her leg. Yanking a condom from his pocket, he slid it on then lifted Avery and held her against the wall as he lowered her onto his thick cock, moaning as he filled her. His hips flexed and pressed into her before pulling out almost all the way, only to thrust deep into her again, moving in a quick staccato.

Avery threw her head back, slamming it into the wall, and gasped Jacob's name as her nails dug into his shoulders. He nipped at her bottom lip then sucked her tongue into his mouth, a low growl rumbling through his chest.

She came with a keening cry, her walls clenching around him. He thrust into her several more times, clutching and clawing at each other as pleasure consumed them.

As the sensations faded, Jacob used his body to hold her against the wall, kissing her. They clung to each other, breathless. He pushed a hand through her messy, blonde hair, kissed the tip of her nose, and set her on her feet.

"Are we good?"

Avery nodded. "Yeah, we're good."

He helped Avery gather her clothes, then he buttoned his pants and grabbed a sweatshirt from the closet.

"I'm hungry. Are you?" he asked.

Avery's lips pursed and her nose wrinkled. "Oh god, no. The thought of food makes me want to puke."

Jacob laughed and shook his head. "I'm not surprised. You had a lot to drink last night. How about some coffee?"

"I could drink coffee." She followed him into the kitchen and eased into a kitchen chair. She folded her arms on the table, laid her head down, and didn't move until he set the cup in front of her.

"Thank you," she mumbled, lifting her head long enough to take a sip before dropping it back to the table.

"Can I talk to you about something?"

"Hm?" She didn't look up.

"Would you be interested in tutoring a group of my freshmen?" Jacob sat down beside her and pushed her hair away from her face.

Avery turned her head and looked up at him. "How many?"

"I think there are seven of them. It would be two hours, once a week, whatever you want. It pays twenty-five dollars an hour." He rubbed her back, observing her. "What do you think?"

She sat up, tucked her hair behind her ear, and cradled her coffee in both hands. "I could use the money. Why are you asking me? Pity or something?"

"No," Jacob chuckled. "You're one of my best students, sweetheart. I looked at your transcripts, and your grades are phenomenal—aside from freshman year. I think you'd make a great tutor. You don't have to decide right now. Just think about it and let me know."

"I don't need to think about it. I can do it." Avery propped her head on her hand. "So, you're spying on me? Checking my transcripts?"

Jacob narrowed his eyes. "I check all of my students' transcripts. I want to see where they stand academically. It helps me be a better teacher."

"Hm, and it helps you check up on the woman you're sleeping with, too, right?"

"Okay, maybe a little." Jacob laughed. "But I swear I look at everyone's grades. I'm not being weird or stalkerish, I swear."

Avery kissed the corner of his mouth and smiled. "Thank God. I don't think I could handle a stalker, not even you. Too freaky."

Chapter 13

Avery

Avery parked in the student lot, wrapped a scarf around her neck, put on her hat, shoved open the car door, and hurried across the lawn to the library. The study group she agreed to tutor met once a week for the rest of the semester. Once inside, she headed straight for the information desk.

It took a second to place the student librarian behind the counter—Becky Small, the irritated girl from Jacob's class the previous week who tried and failed to flirt with Professor Moore. As soon as she glanced up, the warm smile on her face turned to ice. When Avery inquired where the study groups were, Becky gave her a snotty, clipped answer, directing her to the third floor. Ignoring Becky's impudence, Avery raced up the stairs and down the hall, finding the group of freshmen in a small room tucked in the back corner of the third floor.

She slipped inside, her eyes on the floor, mumbling apologies for her lateness as she took the empty seat at the head of the table. She dropped her backpack to the floor and turned to the group. Her eyes landed on Professor Jacob Moore.

Avery swallowed back a startled squeak and cleared her throat. "Professor Moore, what a surprise."

"Ms. Collins, how kind of you to show up."

She narrowed her eyes and gave him a wry smile. "My apologies. It won't happen again." She took a deep breath and tipped her head to one side. "I'm sorry. I didn't realize you would be here."

"I thought I would come to the first study session. While I'm sure you are more than capable, I wanted to make sure everyone was on the right track. Pretend I'm not here."

Avery nodded. "I'd appreciate any insight you might give us."

Two hours later, the group was getting restless and so was she. Pretending Jacob wasn't in the room proved difficult, especially with his eyes following her every move. She checked her watch. The library was about to close. She quickly wrapped things up, scheduled the next study session, and sent everyone on their way.

Once the room emptied of freshman, Avery stacked the books on the table and tossed the garbage in the trash receptacle, all while glancing at her professor out of the corner of her eye. She leaned against the table beside him when she finished.

"What are you doing here, Professor Moore?"

Jacob chuckled, a bemused expression on his face. He stood in front of her and placed his hands on the table around her, caging her in. "I wanted to see you."

She stared, drinking him in. He wore a pair of worn jeans and a greenish-blue shirt, the color intensifying the green of his eyes. He must not have known the effect he had on her—or anyone else—no idea how his smile lit up any room, or how he drew admiring stares everywhere he went, including his classroom. She still couldn't believe he was with her.

"You wanted to see me?"

He nodded. "Yeah." Then he kissed her—a sweet thing that demanded nothing but promised so much.

He pulled away and Avery whined, wanting more.

"You are a fantastic tutor," he said. "I think you deserve to be rewarded."

Jacob's hands slipped beneath her shirt and up her sides as his lips moved over her neck, kissing and nipping at her throat. His thumb brushed across her nipple over her lace bra. She arched her back, pushing her breasts into his hands. His lips closed on the spot where her neck met her shoulder, biting and sucking, marking her. He popped open the button on her jeans and eased his hand past the waistband, his fingers sliding teasingly through her damp folds.

"Jacob," she gasped. "Someone might see us."

He cut off her protests with a kiss before pushing her against the edge of the table and holding her in place as he pressed open-mouthed kisses on her bare skin. She tingled everywhere, heat flooding her.

Jacob dropped to his knees in front of her and placed his warm lips on her stomach. He pulled off her shoes, tossing them aside one at a time. He hooked his fingers in the belt loops on her jeans and eased them down, kissing her bare legs as he went.

He looked up at her with a smirk, his green eyes dark with lust as he pulled one of her legs over his shoulder and nuzzled his nose into the curls at the apex of his thighs, groaning deep in the back of his throat. His tongue flicked out to lick her, circling her clit until her thighs trembled uncontrollably. Jacob slid his hands up the back of Avery's thighs and cupped her ass, holding her tight as he slipped his tongue into her, rolling it over and through her slick pussy. His tongue fucked into her at a maddening pace, his beard burning her inner thighs.

She gasped when his middle finger slipped in alongside his tongue, twisting and pressing the tiny nub of nerves, sending shots of intense, mind-boggling electricity screaming through her body.

The tightly wound coil in the pit of her stomach contracted, and her back arched as her fingers twisted in Jacob's hair, holding him close. Her hips came off the table to meet his mouth, a filthy curse leaving her as the orgasm rushed through her, every nerve in her body on fire with intense pleasure.

Jacob worked Avery through the orgasm, holding her in place so she wouldn't collapse, only pushing himself to his feet when the trembling in her body subsided. He caught her lips in his, still wet with her slick.

Avery hurried to release him from the confines of his jeans, pushing them down enough to take him in her hand and stroke his length. He slid a condom on, then she lifted her hips and guided him to her entrance, moaning as he slid into her.

He nuzzled the side of her neck and groaned as her nails sank into his ass, yanking him closer, urging him to move. With a growl, he tangled his fingers in her hair, tipping her head back and kissing her neck. He thrust into her, hard and deep, hitting her sweet spot with every tilt of his hips. His body tensed, and his hand tightening in her hair as he came, gasping her name.

Jacob pushed her shirt up, dropped his head to take her breast in his mouth, and sucked her nipple through the lacy fabric of her bra. He slipped a hand between their bodies and massaged her clit until she came with a desperate groan.

Avery clung to Jacob for a few minutes to catch her breath, her head resting on his shoulder. He tucked her hair behind her ear and kissed her temple.

"We should go, huh?" he said.

"I think that's a good idea."

Jacob helped her to her feet and back into her clothes, stopping for a moment to glance at the door and the dark library beyond.

"What's wrong?"

"Nothing." He shook his head. "I thought I saw someone. Probably a shadow playing tricks with my imagination." He pulled her into a quick hug and kissed her again. "Come back to my place?"

She nodded. "I'll meet you there."

Jacob squeezed her hand before slipping out the door. She shoved her things into her bag, stopping to catch her breath before she opened the door, and made her way through the eerily dark library.

Outside, fresh snow fell from above, covering the cars in a soft, white blanket. She scanned the lot, but Jacob's car was nowhere to be seen. He must have parked in the faculty lot in the back. It would explain why she hadn't seen his car when she arrived. A loud clanging noise behind her made her jump. She whipped around but she saw nothing. A security guard appeared at the door, just as confused as she was. Avery waved at him and hurriedly climbed in her car, grateful it started on the first try. She put it in gear and pulled out of the lot, driving carefully through the falling snow to Jacob's house.

Chapter 14

Jacob

*J*acob hovered in the state between awake and asleep where everything felt like a dream yet wasn't. He wasn't sure if his phone vibrated or if he imagined it. It stopped after a few seconds, allowing him to dive back into dreamland, but it wasn't quiet for long. The multitude of vibrations sent it across the bedside table. He grabbed it, intent on turning it off, but the first few words of the text caught his eye.

[Unknown: Stop seeing her or I...]

He eased Avery onto her back and tucked the covers around her before he slipped out of bed, yanked on a t-shirt and sweats, and headed downstairs. In his office with the door closed, he opened the text message with shaking hands.

[Unknown: Stop seeing her or I will send these to Charles Ross.]

These were blurry pictures of him and Avery in the library earlier, one of them with his head between her legs, her head thrown back in ecstasy and fingers tangled in his hair. Another showed him buried to the hilt inside of her, a look of pure pleasure on his face. There were seven pictures total.

White fiery anger rushed through him. His vision turned crimson, and his ears rang. He squeezed the phone until the glass screen cracked then chucked it across the room with a strangled growl, watching it hit the couch and bounce to the floor with an unsatisfying thud.

Jacob dropped into his office chair, his head in his hands. He had no idea who sent the photos; he didn't recognize the number. He considered waking Avery but decided against it. She might as well get a few minutes of peace before he dropped this bombshell on her.

—

Avery stood in the middle of his living room, twisting her hands and pacing. Jacob sat a few feet away, his head resting against the back of the couch, eyes closed. He had said little since he'd woken her to show her the photo; he let her rant and rave, watching her anger turn from fear to confusion and finally dejection.

"Come here." He held his hand out.

She crossed the room and let him pull her into his arms.

He pressed his lips to her temple. "Are you sure you don't recognize the number?" he asked.

"I'm sure. What do you think they want?"

"Whoever it is wants me to quit seeing you. Why else would they threaten to send the pictures to Charlie?

Maybe it gives them some kind of sick thrill knowing they have a hold over us."

"This is so stupid," she grumbled. "Who the hell do they think they are?"

Her body tensed in his arms, and her hands clenched into tight fists on her lap. The anger had returned. She twisted out of his grip, shoved to her feet, and resumed her pacing, muttering under her breath.

Jacob rested his elbows on his knees. "I'm sorry about all of this, sweetheart."

She spun around, blonde hair tumbling over her face. "What are you sorry for?"

He scrubbed a hand over the back of his neck and sighed. "This is my fault. I never should have put you in this position. I lose my mind when I'm around you, and I can't think straight. I should have waited, walked away when I had the chance, left you alone—"

"Is that what you want? You don't want to see me any-more? Do you...do you regret us?"

Jacob shot to his feet and pulled Avery into his arms. "Hell, no." He cupped her chin in his hand. "Look at me, sweetheart. I do not, nor will I *ever*, regret us. I wish all of this were easy. I wish I could tell the world how I feel about you." He pushed her hair away from her face and kissed the corner of her mouth. "God, I'm an idiot. If I weren't so selfish, maybe this would never have happened."

Avery shook her head, clinging to him. "It doesn't matter now. None of it matters. All we have to worry about is what we do from here on." She exhaled shakily. "What *are* we going to do?"

Jacob released her, spun on his heel, and took over pacing the room. "Maybe we should lay low for a while.

Keep everything strictly student and teacher until we figure out who is behind the pictures. We shouldn't be alone together or do anything that might look questionable."

Avery perched on the edge of the couch and nodded. The pain in her eyes screamed at him.

He knelt in front of her and rubbed her arms. "I hate it, too, sweetheart. But I don't think we have any choice. I could lose my job and my tenure, everything I've worked for since high school. The college could suspend you, maybe even stop you from getting your degree."

"You're right, of course." She sighed. Avery rose to her feet and eased past him to grab her coat from the back of the chair and picked up her backpack. She didn't look at Jacob as she dug her keys out of her bag.

Jacob grabbed her arm, stopping her before she could get out the door. He wasn't about to let her leave upset, wondering if she'd ever meant anything to him. He couldn't let that happen.

"Hey," he said. "This doesn't change how I feel about you."

"How do you feel about me, Professor Moore?"

He pressed a kiss to the center of her forehead, the tip of her nose, her cheek, then slid his lips down her jaw to her mouth. He rested his forehead against hers, his eyes closed. Jacob struggled with the words to make this right.

"Avery, I...I don't know what to say."

"Of course, you don't." She pulled free of his embrace and bolted through the house. The kitchen door slammed behind her.

Chapter 15

Avery

The next week dragged along, the dreary weather of early March matching Avery's depressed mood. The day after Jacob received the pictures, she called in sick, told Nat she had the flu, and holed up in her room. She skipped her classes to wallow in her misery and binge-watch *Friends*.

She exchanged a few texts with Jacob, but she kept those to a minimum as well. Every time she talked to him, her heart broke all over again. The constant worry tore her apart. She couldn't sleep or eat and didn't want to leave her room.

Despite her misery, by the time Friday came around, she had to leave the apartment. There was a test in Jacob's class. She'd dreaded it all week—being in the same room as Jacob, breathing the same air, so close yet forced to keep her distance. She considered skipping, but it was the midterm, her last test before spring break started next week.

Avery trudged across the snow-laden campus, her feet as heavy as her heart. Inside, Jacob watched her as she eased down the aisle and slipped into a chair in the top row as far from him as possible. She itched to touch him, to kiss him, to throw herself into his arms, push him into his office, and make love to him on his stupid, ragged, plaid couch. Instead, she kept her head down and busied herself yanking things from her backpack.

Jacob turned his back on the class and wrote on the board. She stared at the back of his head and gnawed on her pen, her stomach twisting and churning. When he turned around and leaned against his desk, she noticed he looked exhausted—his eyes red-rimmed and his hair tousled as if he crawled out of bed after a restless night. But he was still gorgeous.

"Alright folks, I've got some good news and some bad news for you." A hint of a smile played across his lips. "The good news is Professor Hess will be back after spring break, so you won't have to look at my ugly mug anymore."

His self-deprecating comment earned him a few laughs. He cleared his throat and continued.

"Now for the bad news. You still have to take the test."

The class groaned in unison, this time making him laugh. He grabbed the papers from his desk and passed them around, looking at Avery several times as he made his way around the room.

Only a few other students were left when she finished her test. She walked to the front of the classroom, set it on Jacob's desk, and turned to leave.

"Excuse me, Ms. Collins?"

Avery stopped short. The sound of her name in his deep voice sent a tingle down her spine. An ache built low in her gut.

"Yes, Professor Moore?" She locked eyes with Jacob.

"Have you scheduled another study session with my freshman group?"

Avery nodded. "I'm meeting with them Monday night. The test is next Wednesday, right?"

"Yes," he replied, staring at the floor for a few seconds. When he looked up, he had a hopeful expression on his face. "I wanted to ask you something. I was...uh, wondering if you...do you have a minute?" He pushed himself to his feet and pointed at his office door.

Avery shook her head. "I'm sorry. I have to get home." She spun on her heel, sprinted up the stairs, grabbed her coat and backpack on the run, and burst out the door, ignoring Jacob shouting after her. She didn't stop until she was outside. Assaulted by the stinging cold, she tugged on her jacket before hurrying across the parking lot.

Then stopped dead in her tracks. Her car leaned oddly to one side as if it was off balance. A large screwdriver protruded from the front driver's side tire. The passenger's side tire was deflated, a slash gaping across the rubber. A folded piece of paper fluttered under the windshield wipers. She plucked it free and took a deep breath before opening it.

Stay away from Jacob. Or next time it will be more than your tires that I slash.

———

"Drink this." Jacob pushed a hot mug into her hands.

Avery took a sip, wincing as the alcohol in the cup burned her throat. She blew out a shaky breath and closed her eyes. As soon as she pulled the cryptic note off her car, she had sprinted back across campus, ignoring her burning lungs as fear clutched wildly at her heart and drove her forward.

She burst through Jacob's office door, tears streaming down her face, babbling incoherently, and waving the note in his face. It took him several minutes to calm her down and figure out what happened.

Avery took another drink of the burning whiskey. She coughed, set it on the table, and hugged herself. She couldn't stop shivering. Dragging in a deep breath, she took her phone from her bag.

"I think we should call the police," she said.

"The police?"

"I know someone we can call," Avery explained. "A friend in the sheriff's department."

"You think that's a good idea?"

Avery nodded. "I do. Why? You don't?"

"I didn't say that," he huffed. "I just... this is gonna—" His mouth snapped closed, and he swallowed, his throat clicking. He exhaled and scratched the back of his neck. "Make the call."

Jacob sat beside her as she called. He listened as she explained what happened. When she disconnected the call, he tipped his head to the side, one eyebrow raised.

"Well?"

"My friend, Brent, is a sheriff's deputy. He'll be here soon to take our statements."

Less than ten minutes later, Brent Taft, her ex-boy-friend—if you could call him that—stepped through the door, his hat pulled low over his eyes, and his hand resting on the butt of the gun at his hip.

"Professor Moore?"

Jacob nodded and stepped around the table, his hand extended. Brent glanced at it and turned away. The deputy looked at Avery curiously. "Hello, Avery."

"Hey, Brent."

She and Brent went out two or three times, but there was no chemistry. They'd parted ways amicably, though she sometimes suspected that Brent's feelings were much deeper than hers had been. On the few occasions they'd crossed paths, she caught him looking at her with a longing that made her uncomfortable.

"What can I do for you folks?" Brent asked.

After a slight hesitation, Jacob told the deputy about the photos sent via text and the threatening note left on Avery's car. They spent the better part of an hour talking. When he left, Brent had the photos from Jacob's phone and a list of people who might have taken them: one of Avery's former roommates, an old boyfriend, and some students Jacob knew had a mischievous side. It impressed her that Brent maintained a professional demeanor; he only gave her a disapproving look once or twice. He seemed to reserve his irritation for Jacob, his questions clipped and accusatory.

"Deputy Taft?" Avery interrupted Brent's third repeat of the same question. "I'd like to go home, if there isn't anything else you need?" She glared at the deputy, hoping he got the hint. Enough was enough.

"Yes, ma'am," Brent said. He picked up the note, folded it in half, then in half again. He slipped it in his pocket and turned to Avery.

"I promise I will figure out who did this to you, Avery. You don't deserve to be tormented. Okay?"

"O-okay," she stammered. She didn't care for the expression on his face—oddly hopeful. "Can I ask you a favor?"

"Of course. Whatever I can do."

"Can you please keep this confidential? I know it has to go in the police report—"

"I'll tell you what," the deputy interrupted. "I'll wait a few days to file the official report, see if I can get some leads before I bring Sheriff Willis into the loop. Okay?"

The tension left Avery's body. "That would be great. Thank you."

Jacob walked Taft to his office door, shook his hand, and closed the door behind him. He exhaled loudly, crossed the room, and sat beside Avery on the couch. Taking her hand, he held it loosely, his shoulder touching hers.

"You should come back to my place tonight," he insisted. "I don't want you to go home alone."

"I wouldn't be alone," she scoffed. "Nat's there. Besides, we're lying low, remember?" She heard the frustration in her voice and immediately regretted it.

Jacob slipped an arm around her waist, his nose brushing against her cheek, his lips a breath away from hers. "I can't do this anymore. I don't want this...this guillotine hanging over our heads. I'm going to the university president."

"Jacob, you don't—"

He cut her off, his mouth slanting over hers. The kiss made Avery ache with need, hope bursting in her chest.

"I'll explain everything—how we met, how you're only my student because of Hess's leave of absence, all of it."

"And then what?"

"I beg Charlie not to fire me. Pray he lets me keep my job and my reputation isn't destroyed." Jacob rubbed the back of his neck and stared at the floor.

"I don't want you to do that," she said. She pushed to her feet and stood in front of him. "Let's see if Brent can do anything. Maybe you won't have to go to Ross."

Jacob sighed and stood up from the couch. He pulled her close, his warmth seeping into her. He brushed a kiss across her lips and rested his forehead against hers.

"I miss you, sweetheart."

"I miss you, too. I hate this. But please, Jacob, don't do anything crazy. Not yet. Promise me you'll wait."

Jacob closed his eyes and nodded. "I promise."

Avery sighed. She wasn't sure she believed him. "We can wait a few days, right?"

"I think so." He gave her a wry smile and kissed her again. "Call me when you get home?"

She nodded, hugging him close a moment longer, inhaling his scent, before she grabbed her stuff and hurried from the room, wiping tears from her cheeks.

Chapter 16

Jacob

Jacob promised Avery he wouldn't go to Charlie until Deputy Taft investigated who was behind the pictures and the note. He didn't like it, but he'd promised. Problem was he wasn't sure how long he could keep that promise. He wanted this to end. He wanted Avery.

Exhausted, he went home early, ate some leftover Chinese food, and drank a couple of beers. He tried watching TV, but he couldn't find anything interesting. Too many things crowded his brain.

He fell asleep on the couch fully dressed, his jacket shoved under his head, and one of his mother's afghans thrown over his legs. His dreams were memories of the last couple of days interspersed with whatever television show played in the background.

He slept like shit and woke when the sunlight shone through the thin curtains of his living room. He threw the blanket off and sat up, digging his fingers into the tight knots in the back of his neck.

He grabbed his phone and scrolled through his notifications. There was a lengthy voicemail from Avery.

"You're probably asleep, but I can't keep this in. I have to tell you. I hate this, Jacob. I hate not being able to be with you. I've tried to convince myself that we're nothing more than two people having fun. I told myself this is nothing more than a clandestine affair with my teacher." She giggled, and her voice dropped to a whisper. "This is so much more than a crazy, meaningless affair. I...I love you, Jacob." Another giggle followed by a loud sigh. "I can't believe I told you I love you over voicemail. How ridiculous am I? Don't answer that. I've been drinking, as if you couldn't tell. Shit. You know what, call me tomorrow, okay?"

Jacob stared at the phone in his hand. Jesus Christ, she *loved* him. The question was, did he love her?

It took him about five seconds to decide; he loved her, had for a while now, but he was afraid to admit it to himself, let alone to her. He'd let his fear get in the way.

Jacob was in too deep to turn back.

He regretted nothing. He never would. The more he thought about it, the more he knew what he had to do. He swiped his finger across the screen of his phone, pulled up his contacts, and dialed.

———

"Jacob, hi." Serena smiled at him from her desk. "How are things going?"

"Eh, not bad," he replied, shrugging a shoulder. "It's good to see you, again. How's Van?"

Serena's smile widened, and she blushed. "He's good. Enjoying his new gig as the head of security."

Jacob laughed. "He's enjoying it?"

"He said he's having fun. And I swear these damn college kids love him." She scrunched her nose and shook her head. "Especially the girls."

"You have nothing to worry about." Jacob chuckled. "Van loves you. Spend half an hour talking to him, and you'll know."

Serena giggled and pushed away from her desk. "Let me ask Charlie if he's ready to see you."

"Hey, wait. What kind of mood is he in?"

She paused in front of Charlie's door and lowered her voice. "Um, he's kind of grumpy. He's not happy about coming in on Saturday. I hope whatever you need to talk to him about won't piss him off."

"It might," Jacob groaned.

"Great," she mumbled. She took a deep breath and gave Jacob a less-than-cheerful look. "Give me a minute." She disappeared through a heavy oak door into an inner office, her "hey, Charlie" drifting over her shoulder as it swung shut.

Jacob sank into a plush chair against the wall. Out of the corner of his eye, he glimpsed a photo on Serena's desk—a picture of her, Van, and their dog, Soldier. He was looking forward to their wedding this summer.

Thinking about weddings reminded him it had been a while since he talked to Luke. He made a mental note to call his best friend.

He clasped his hands between his legs, his knuckles aching and hands clammy. His stomach rolled. He wanted this to be over. Charlie was a good guy, a great boss, and a hard-ass about his university's reputation. Nobody got away with improprieties on his watch.

Jacob pushed a hand through his hair, his knee bouncing, his brain creating all sorts of weird scenarios about this meeting. Most involved him getting fired.

The door opened, and Serena stepped out. "He'll see you now."

Charlie sat behind his desk, a faint smile on his face. Once Jacob sat down and Serena closed the door, Charlie tossed his glasses on the desk, sat back in his chair, and crossed his arms.

"Serena said I might not like this."

"You won't," Jacob replied.

"Let's hear it," Charlie grumbled.

Jacob wasn't sure what to say. He took a deep breath and opened his mouth.

"I'm in love with a student."

The words he hadn't even said to Avery yet jumped out of his mouth on their own, eager to expose themselves. His mouth snapped shut as soon as it was out, and he leaned forward, his elbows on his knees.

"Go on," Charlie said, surprisingly calm.

He stumbled over his own words, unable to explain himself. He struggled to relax, to take his time, otherwise he would screw this up. Jacob sat back in his chair and started from the beginning, the first time he met Avery. By the time he finished, it was as if someone had lifted a weight from his shoulders.

"She's in Hess's class?" Charlie asked, swiveling in his chair.

Jacob nodded. "Yes. Which means she's no longer my student."

"When did you start dating?"

"Over winter break." Short, honest answers, no extraneous information. Charlie wouldn't want to hear it.

Charlie scrubbed a hand over his face. "You didn't know she was a student when you asked her out?"

"No," Jacob mumbled. "We met at The Percolator; she works there. I didn't know she was a student. I never asked, either. Not very smart."

"Damn right it wasn't smart," Charlie snapped, pushing himself to his feet. "You live and work in a college town, Jacob. Most of the town's population either works at or goes to the university."

"Yes, sir."

"Maybe you didn't ask because you didn't want to know."

Jacob cringed. Charlie was right. He looked at his boss and shrugged.

Charlie stopped pacing behind his desk and leaned over it, his palms flat on the surface. "I need some time to think things over. This is a complicated situation, Jacob. Not just because you're a professor and she's a student. You're esteemed in your field. This could be an enormous scandal neither one of us needs. Thank you for coming to me before it blew up in our faces." He dropped back into his chair, put his glasses on, and grabbed his tablet. "I'll call you tomorrow or Monday at the latest. Until then, don't do anything stupid." He looked at Jacob over his glasses. "That will be all, Professor Moore."

"Yes, sir," Jacob muttered, launching from the chair and striding out the door. He shouted goodbye to Serena over his shoulder as he hurried from the office.

At the bottom of the stairs, three floors down, he leaned against the wall, hands on his knees, panting as he tried to catch his breath. He took his phone from his pocket and dialed from memory, a smile spreading across his face when she answered.

It was the definition of stupid, and it flew in the face of everything Charlie said. But he needed to tell her what he'd done. It would affect her life as much as his.

———

As soon as Jacob pulled to a stop in front of Avery's apartment building, the front door opened and Avery appeared, a smile pasted on her face. She yanked open the door, climbed inside, clasped her hands together, and cleared her throat.

"Hi," she said.

"Hi, sweetheart." He wrapped a hand around the back of her neck, pulled her close, and brushed his lip across hers.

"I thought we were lying low."

Jacob rested his forehead against hers. "I had to see you." He released her and put the car in gear. They drove to his place in comfortable silence, her hand in his.

Once they were at his house, the curtains drawn, a glass of wine in Avery's hand, and a beer in his, he was ready to talk. He wrapped his arm around her shoulders, hugging her close, and pressed his lips to her temple.

"I have to tell you something."

Her voice shook when she spoke. "What is it?"

"I met with Charlie today. Charles Ross."

"The university president?" she asked. "We agreed you'd wait."

Jacob rubbed his hand over the back of his neck and sat forward, his elbows on his knees, his beer held loosely in his hand. He stared across the room at the TV. "I decided not to wait."

She set her wine on the table and wrapped her arms around herself, her face ashen. Her lower lip trembled. "I don't understand."

"I had to do something. Whoever is threatening us has too much power over us. I had to take that away. So, I went to Charlie and told him everything."

Avery slipped off the couch and kneeled between his legs, her hands resting on his thighs. "What happened?" she asked.

Jacob shrugged. "It was anticlimactic. He said he needed time to think things over and he'd call me tomorrow or Monday. Until then, I'm not supposed to do anything stupid."

"Your idea of not doing anything stupid is to call me, pick me up at my place, and bring me back here?"

He set his beer on the table, cupped her face, and pressed a hard kiss to her lips. "I told you, I needed to see you."

"What is Ross going to do?"

"I don't know," he admitted.

"This is all my fault," she muttered. "If I hadn't fallen in love—"

"This is on both of us. You can't help who you're attracted to. You can't help who you fall in love with. If I had to do it again, I would still get your phone number, and I would still ask you out." He squeezed her hands. "I would still fall in love with you."

Avery drew in a sharp breath and tears filled her eyes. "You love me?"

"Yes, I love you. I'm sorry I didn't say it sooner. I'm an idiot. I'm not making decisions based on what other people want. I'd give up everything if it meant being with you." He pulled her into his arms, kissing her neck as he hugged her against his chest.

"Can I ask you something?"

"Anything," Jacob said and stroked her hair, twisting the blonde curls around his fingers.

"You didn't do this because you're colossally stupid, right? You did it because you love me and can't live without me?"

Even though there was a playful quality to her question, he could see the underlying fear and worry in her gorgeous brown eyes. He hugged her tight, his lips pressed to her ear.

"I love you, and I can't live without you, sweetheart," he whispered. "I promise we'll figure it out. We'll make this work, no matter what Charlie says."

Chapter 17

Jacob

Late Monday afternoon, Jacob's phone rang, the sound shrill and jarring in the quiet of his office. He dropped his pen and snatched the handset.

"Professor Moore," he answered.

"Jacob? It's Serena. Are you available to come by and see Charlie?"

His heart skipped a beat, and he couldn't quite catch his breath. He swallowed back the fear rising in his throat and mumbled, "Yes."

Serena told him to come by in an hour. He hung up the phone with shaking hands, sat down in his office chair, then sent a text to Avery to let her know he was meeting with Charlie. She responded with a heart emoji and a reminder to tell her everything as soon as he could.

There was a chill in the air despite spring being weeks away. Jacob shoved his hands in his pockets as he trudged through the light snow covering the ground.

He was almost at the administration offices when his cell phone vibrated. He waited until he was in the building before taking it out of his pocket.

[Avery: I haven't heard from Brent. Still trying to reach him. Will let you know when I do. Have you seen Ross yet?]

[Jacob: I'm about to go in. What are you doing?]

[Avery: I'm at the coffee shop. Ruby needs help. Jules is out sick.]

[Jacob: Call me when you're off. I'll let you know what Ross says. Wish me luck.]

Avery sent him heart emojis along with a devil, which made him laugh. He tucked his phone in his pocket, tapped on the office door, and stepped inside.

Serena rose to her feet, a smile on her face as she came out from behind her desk to shake Jacob's hand.

"He's waiting for you," she said, pointing at Charlie's office door.

"Has he said anything to you?" Jacob asked.

She shook her head. "He's playing this one close to the vest. Come on." Serena opened the door and ushered him inside, giving him one last smile before stepping back out.

Jacob took a seat, leaned forward, and rested his elbows on his knees. His foot tapped incessantly until Charlie shot a look in his direction.

"Thanks for coming by, Jacob. You know, this hasn't made my life easy. I spent the entire weekend worrying about this."

"And?" Jacob asked.

"I'm not firing you. But you are on probation until further notice. If you screw up again, I will fire you. Understood?"

Jacob breathed a little easier. "Yes, sir."

"As for your relationship with Ms. Collins, I will not forbid it. To my unending surprise, it is not against the rules. There is no specific rule against fraternization between professors and students; the handbook merely suggests it *could* be inappropriate. But you and Ms. Collins are close in age, and you are no longer her professor, so it skirts the inappropriate suggestion. I am going to ask you to do your best to keep the relationship low-key. Can you do that?"

Jacob nodded. "Yes, sir."

A faint smile danced across Charlie's face. "You're lucky I like you, Jacob. And I did owe you one for taking over Hess's class. I didn't expect anything like this, though. Do me a favor and don't run around campus making a spectacle of yourselves, okay?"

"We won't," Jacob replied. "I promise."

"I'm holding you to that. Thank you again for bringing this to me before things got out of control."

"You're welcome, Mr. Ross. I appreciate your under-standing." Jacob rose to his feet, shook Charlie's hand, and scurried out of the office.

On the way back to his office, Jacob decided he would call Deputy Taft himself. If he wouldn't answer Avery, maybe he would answer Jacob's call. As soon as he shut the door behind himself, he looked up the sheriff's number and dialed.

"Sheriff's office, Sheriff Willis speaking."

"Donna? Donna Willis?"

"Um, yes, this is Donna Willis. With whom am I speaking?"

Jacob cleared his throat. Donna graduated high school a couple of years before him; she probably wouldn't even remember him. "Donna, this Jacob Moore. We went to high school together."

"Jacob! Hi! I heard you were back in town. What can I do for you?"

"Is Deputy Taft available? I'd like to speak to him."

There was an awkward silence before Donna spoke. "May I ask what this is regarding?"

"I wanted to ask him if he has made any headway on the case involving myself and Avery Collins?"

"What case?" Donna asked.

Jacob explained the tire slashing and the photographs. Taft must not have told Sheriff Willis yet; he had said he would wait a few days.

"Are you sure it was Taft? Absolutely sure?"

"Yes. Avery called him herself."

Sheriff Willis exhaled. "Jacob, Deputy Taft has been on administrative leave since Christmas. He shouldn't be investigating any cases. Did you call our office to report it?"

"I'm...I'm not sure. Avery called it in—"

There was silence on the other end of the line, silence Jacob didn't like.

"Donna?"

"I'll call you back, Jacob."

Before he could say anything, the line disconnected. He stared at the phone, dumbfounded, before hanging it up. A thick fog invaded his brain. He picked up his cell phone and called Avery. It went straight to voicemail, so he texted her.

[Jacob: Avery. Call me. Now.]

—

Jacob gunned the engine, speeding through the twenty-five mile per hour speed zone in the middle of town. His conversation with Sheriff Willis made him uneasy, and Avery not answering her phone had his head in all the wrong places. He needed to find her.

He stopped in front of the coffee shop, slammed the car into park, and sprinted to the front door, leaving the car running with the door open. He burst into the building, but the coffee shop was empty.

"Avery!" he shouted.

"Jacob! Back here!"

Jacob darted through the swinging door, following the sound of Avery's voice. He caught sight of Avery going out the back door. She glanced back over her shoulder, her overly bright eyes locking on his and her face ashen. He took a step forward, but she was suddenly gone as if she had never been there.

He followed her, stumbling over boxes stacked near the door and knocking them to the floor. He had to get to Avery. The fear in her eyes had chilled him to the bone.

Jacob burst through the door into a short alleyway. Thirty yards up the street, Avery was being dragged toward her car by a man he couldn't make out. The man shoved Avery into her car and climbed in behind her.

"Avery!"

Her brake lights flashed, and the car pulled away from the curb, fishtailing on the damp street.

Chapter 18

Avery

Avery shoved her phone into her purse and shut down the engine. She stared out the windshield. *I shouldn't have told Ruby I would work.* All she would do was worry about Jacob's meeting with Mr. Ross and watch the clock until she could call him. Ruby had a strict "no cell phone" rule when working, so she wouldn't be able to talk to Jacob until she was off.

With an irritated sigh, she pushed open the car door and hurried inside. She snatched her apron off the hook by the door, tucked her silenced phone in her back pocket, dropped her things in the office, and made her way out front.

"Avery, thank God." Ruby pushed a hand through her hair and gave her a weak smile. "You're a lifesaver. Thank you for coming in."

She patted Ruby's arm. "I'm happy to help. Now, don't you need to go? Something about a soccer game?"

"Yes. Carson should be here in less than an hour. Can you handle things until then?"

Avery looked around the empty coffee shop. "Uh, I think so." She laughed and pushed Ruby toward the swinging door leading to the back. "Go, take J.J. to his game."

Ruby yelled goodbye over her shoulder, and a few minutes later, Avery heard the back door slam closed.

"Can I talk to you, Avery?"

She gasped and spun around, one hand grasping the counter to keep from falling.

"Brent! You scared the crap out of me." She leaned against the counter. "I've been trying to call you."

"I know," Deputy Taft said. He glanced over his shoulder then stepped behind the counter. "I have to tell you something."

"Um, okay. Is it…is it about my tires? Or the pictures? Did you find out anything?"

"I don't think you should date Jacob anymore," Brent snarled.

"Wait? What?" Her chest tightened, and sweat dripped down her back.

"You need to stop seeing Jacob. If you don't, I'll have to tell the university."

Realization hit Avery like a hard slap. Brent took the pictures and slashed her tires. She jerked her arms down, gripped the counter behind her, and tried to not to scream.

"I think you should go," she gritted out through her teeth.

"Give me a minute," Brent snapped. "Hear me out."

Avery shook her head. "I don't think we have anything to talk about."

He was right in her face. Avery took a step back but was blocked by the counter. She cleared her throat and inched to the left, hoping she could get around Brent.

Brent's hand closed around her upper arm. "Five minutes, Avery. That's all I'm asking."

Avery shook her head again. "No. You need to go." She tried to pull away, but Brent's grip tightened painfully.

"Please?" Brent begged.

"Let me go." She tried to yank free, but he wouldn't let go.

Brent mumbled something unintelligible under his breath and looked around. After a second, in which she hoped he might give up and let her go, he pushed her through the swinging door and into the back of the shop, ignoring Avery's protests.

"What are you doing?" she cried, struggling against his grip.

"I want to talk to you. I need you to listen to me for five minutes. That's it." His lip curled, his handsome face turning demonic.

Avery's heart pounded, and her entire body shook. Brent dragged her toward the back door. She heard the bell over the front door ring, then Jacob called her name.

"Jacob! Back here!" she yelled.

"Shit." Brent yanked her out the door, but not before she saw Jacob, her eyes locking with his. She whimpered and tried again to yank free, but Brent wasn't letting go. He hustled her down the alley to her car, pushed her into the driver's seat, and climbed in beside her.

"This isn't funny, Brent," she snapped. "Let me out of the car."

Brent popped open the glove box and pulled out her extra set of keys. He dropped them in her lap, reached into his pocket, removed his service revolver, and pressed it against her side. "Start the car and drive, Avery. Now."

She did as she was told, her hands shaking as she put the car in gear and hit the gas, the ass end of the car fish-tailing as she accelerated on the wet street.

———

Avery swiped at the tears sliding down her cheek and gnawed on her lower lip, the faint coppery taste of blood on her tongue. She didn't want Brent to hear her cry. He'd been babbling on since they left The Percolator, telling her why she had to break up with Jacob and give him another shot.

The depth of his obsession with her sank in as they drove. He knew everything: how she met Jacob, how many times they'd gone out over the winter break, even the first time they had sex. It was obvious he'd been watching her. Following her. Stalking her. Fear crawled over her, bringing goosebumps to the surface of her skin.

"Turn there." Brent pointed at a barely visible dirt road up ahead, a mere gap in the trees.

She turned and followed the seldom-used road, the car bouncing and dipping on the dirt tracks. It ended two hundred yards into the trees. She stopped the car, put it in park, and left the engine running.

Oppressive silence filled the car, thickening the air with tension. Avery cleared her throat and turned to Brent with a watery smile.

"What are we doing out here, Brent?" She tried to keep her tone pleasant and accommodating, scared she would anger the sheriff's deputy if she didn't stay calm.

"I told you—I wanted to talk to you." He pushed the gun hard into her stomach.

Her smile wavered, but she did her best to hold it in place. "What do you want to talk about?"

"You and Jacob. The two of you, you're not...you're not meant to be. But you and me, we are."

Avery shook her head before she could stop herself. The look Brent gave her made skin crawl. She swallowed back the biting remark on her lips.

Brent's eyes narrowed, but he continued. "I know it's hard to understand, but *our* lives are meant to intersect, *our* lives are meant to be joined. We will be together. I will do anything I have to to make that happen."

"Brent, we only went out a couple of times—"

"That doesn't matter!" He slammed his fist down on the dashboard, leaving a considerable dent.

Avery slapped her hand over her mouth and cowered against the door, her eyes on the gun.

"When I saw you in the library...when I saw what *he* was doing to you, my anger got the best of me. I was going to go to the university and tell them, even if it meant Jacob losing his job or you getting kicked out of school." Brent scrubbed a hand over his face. "But then I realized maybe I could make you break up, which would give me a chance to prove to you I am the person you belong with. If you would just try to understand, then I could breathe again. I could *live* again."

Anger flooded her. "So, this is what you do?" she yelled. "You kidnap me and drag me to the middle of nowhere? You think this is going to make me want to be with you?"

"Avery, just listen to me—"

"I listened to you, Brent. I listened to you tell me you've been following me, obsessing over me, and you tried to blackmail me into dating you. That's what I heard."

Brent sighed and shook his head. "You never gave me a chance. You broke up with me and forgot about me."

"That's not true."

"Stop. Don't patronize me." He moved the gun, pulling it away from her side to set it on the seat between his legs, his hand resting on his thigh, inches from the weapon. "If you'd just given me a chance, maybe things would be different."

Speechless, Avery shifted restlessly in her seat. The corner of her phone jabbed her in the ass. She'd forgotten it was in her pocket. She glanced at Brent out of the corner of her eye, but he was staring out the passenger window, muttering incoherently under his breath.

Without taking time to think, Avery shoved open her door and threw herself on the ground. She scrambled to her feet and took off at a dead run, not sure where she was going. All she knew was she needed to get away from Brent. She heard a pop and felt a sharp sting on her right arm then a warm gush, but she kept running. With another pop, she felt her hair move as a bullet sailed past her and hit the tree a foot to her left. She ducked, fell to her knees, and crawled into the brush. Low to the ground, she crawled on her hands and knees through the trees, rocks embedding into her hands and branches scraping her arms and face, until she couldn't hear Brent anymore. Only then did she stand up and start running again, her hand pressed to the bleeding wound on her arm. She checked to make sure her phone was still in her pocket and sent up a quick prayer that it would work this deep in the woods.

It has to work. It has to.

Chapter 19

Jacob

Jacob sat in the corner, a steaming cup of coffee in front of him. He watched Sheriff Willis on the other side of the room talking with Ruby. He glanced at his watch; it had been two hours since Avery disappeared with Deputy Taft. Sitting here doing nothing was killing him.

"Professor Moore?" Sheriff Willis slipped into the seat across from him.

He gave her a weary smile. "You can call me Jacob, Sheriff."

"Only if you call me Donna." She set her notebook on the table and cleared her throat. "Is it okay if I ask you a few questions?"

Jacob bit his tongue and nodded. Donna shouldn't be here asking questions; she should be looking for Avery. He rubbed the center of his forehead and forced himself to be patient.

"How long have you two been seeing each other?"

"Since winter break," he responded. "So, what's that? Three months."

Donna scribbled in her notebook, her eyebrows scrunched together. She did that in high school when concentrating.

"When did you receive the photos you told me about?"

"Um, I guess about two, two-and-a-half weeks ago."

"And when did Miss Collins call Deputy Taft?"

He was sure of this answer. "A week and two days ago after she found her tires slashed. She came back to my office and called him from there. We both assumed he filed the report and the incident was being investigated."

"I can't tell you how sorry I am." Donna sighed. "I suspended him in December. I wrongly assumed he wouldn't do anything stupid, so I didn't take his badge or service revolver. Rookie mistake. But we are doing everything in our power to find her."

"Who is *we*, Sheriff?" Jacob snorted. "I've seen you and Taft. So that leaves you."

"I have two other deputies I've pulled in, along with the state police. I promise you we will find her. And we'll find Deputy Taft."

"Sheriff Willis?"

A young, female deputy stopped a foot away from the table, a hand on the butt of her gun, the other on her hip. She didn't look old enough to drink, let alone carry a weapon.

Donna excused herself, patting Jacob on the arm as she walked past him to join the deputy. They put their heads together and whispered, then hurried out the front door of the shop.

Jacob followed, yanking his jacket on as he pushed through the people crowding the small coffee shop. He stepped out the front door as the sheriff's car flew past, lights on and siren wailing.

Natasha appeared at his side, her face pale, dark circles under her eyes. Her boyfriend—Jacob thought his name was Brick—stood off to one side, arms crossed and glaring at everyone.

"Any word?" Natasha asked.

Jacob shook his head. "No. But Sheriff Willis took off like a bat out of hell. I don't know why."

Natasha wrapped her arms around herself. "You know, Avery didn't tell me she was seeing you. She usually tells me everything."

Jacob squeezed her shoulder. "We didn't tell anyone. I didn't even tell *my* best friend. It was...*is* complicated."

Natasha shrugged, obviously unconvinced, and wandered off. Jacob scrubbed a hand over the back of his neck and wondered for the millionth time if Avery was okay. This was all his fault. If he hadn't been so stupid...

"They found her." Luke came out of the coffee shop and stopped in front of Jacob. He'd come down as soon as Jacob called him, no questions asked. Luke was incredibly supportive despite his obvious curiosity. It was a temporary reprieve; the third degree would start as soon as Avery was safe.

"What? Where?" Jacob asked.

"An old logging road north of town. She's been wandering the woods for hours, no cell service, alone, hurt, and near hypothermia."

"Hurt?" Jacob snapped. "What do you mean, hurt?"

"I overheard someone say it was a bullet wound. They're taking her to the hospital."

"Shit." Jacob turned and sprinted to his car, gesturing for Luke to follow. He pulled away from the curb before Luke even shut his door.

———

"When can I see her?" Jacob demanded.

The nurse behind the counter rolled his eyes again. "Mr. Moore, you're going to have to be patient. You aren't family or listed as an emergency contact, so I cannot let you back to see her. Not unless she agrees to see you."

Jacob leaned over the counter. "Then go ask her," he snarled.

"She's with the sheriff. Talk to her when she comes out." The nurse spun on his heel and disappeared through a door behind the counter.

Luke grabbed Jacob's arm and dragged him back to the waiting area. "Stop bugging the staff." He pushed Jacob into a chair and sat beside him. "They have enough to worry about without you harassing them."

Jacob slumped in his seat, head in his hands. "You know, you don't have to babysit me."

Luke chuckled. "Apparently, I do. Otherwise, you'll keep bugging that poor nurse."

"I'm serious. Go home to Bonnie. I'm sure she's wondering where you are."

"I doubt it," his friend muttered. "We...well, the wedding is off."

Jacob sat up straight in his seat. "What? You're kidding, right?"

"Nope. We broke up two weeks ago."

Jacob scrubbed a hand over his face. He was a shitty friend. He'd been so wrapped up in his own world and problems that he hadn't realized his friend's life had gone to hell.

"Christ, Luke, I'm so sorry."

Luke shrugged. "I'm okay. I think it's for the best. We weren't good together."

"Why didn't you tell me?" Jacob asked.

"You seemed distracted, worried about something and dealing with your own problems. I didn't want to burden you with mine." Luke smiled. "I guess it was because of Avery, huh?"

"Yeah. I love her. But she's a student. Made it—"

"—complicated," Luke finished. "I think it's time we got a beer and talked. We have a lot to discuss."

"Jacob?" Sheriff Willis—Donna—came out of the emergency room door. "Ms. Collins is asking for you."

He glanced at Luke, who nodded his approval. He jumped to his feet and followed Donna back down the hall.

"How is she?" he asked.

"She got lucky. We found her before the onset of hypothermia. It was close. She has a bullet wound on her arm and scrapes and bruises from running through the woods. She's understandably freaked out from being kidnapped."

"Did you find Taft?"

Donna nodded. "Yes. Lost in the woods, looking for Avery. He's at the station. The state police are processing him, and then they'll take him to Missoula." She stopped in front of a closed curtain and pulled it back.

Avery was on a bed piled high with blankets, her eyes closed, purple circles under her lashes. She stirred and turned, her warm brown eyes locking with Jacob's.

"Hi." Tears welled in her eyes. She held out her hands to him.

Jacob strode past Donna to sit on the side of the bed. He took Avery's face in his hands, tilting it back to examine the scratches and bruises, his thumb brushing over her lips. He closed his eyes and kissed her forehead. She sagged against the pillows, the tears sliding down her face.

"I'm so sorry, baby," he said, holding her close and stroking her hair.

He held her until she stopped trembling and her tears dried up, then he tucked the blanket around her and rose to his feet. "I should let you get some rest." He swept her hair behind her ear and kissed her.

Avery grabbed his hand, squeezing it so tight her knuckles turned white. "Don't leave." Panic laced her words. "Please, Jacob. Stay with me."

She didn't have to ask twice. Jacob wasn't sure he'd ever be able to leave her again. He stretched out on the bed and wrapped his arms around her, careful not to jostle the IV in her arm. She rested her head on his chest and closed her eyes. Within minutes, she was asleep in his arms.

Chapter 20

Avery

"How'd it go yesterday?" Nat dropped her backpack in the booth and slid in.

"It sucked," Avery replied. "Thank God Jacob was with me. I was a wreck. Testifying in front of a grand jury is nerve-wracking. But I don't have to see Brent again until the trial. Unless the asshole pleads guilty."

"Do you think he'll do that?"

Avery shook her head. "No. Jacob thinks it will go to trial. I just want it to be over. I want them to find Brent guilty and put him in jail. I only wish it could be for the rest of his life."

Nat took Avery's hand and clasped it between hers. "Me too, kiddo. Me too. That jerk deserves it after what he did to you."

"Let's change the subject, okay?"

Nat laughed and dropped her hands. "Sure. How goes the job hunt?"

Avery crossed her eyes and stuck out her tongue. "That sucks, too. I think I might have found something with the high school up in Kalispell. I'm waiting to hear from the principal. What about you?"

"Say hello to the newest member, co-director, stage manager, and head of marketing for the Lakeside Thespians Dinner Theatre." Nat jumped to her feet and curtsied with a grand sweep of her arms.

"Aw, Nat, that's awesome! I'm so jealous."

"Don't be." Nat giggled, returning to her seat. "It's not as grand as it sounds. But the theatre is under new management, and they hope to make a name for themselves. They have big plans for the summer and the influx of tourists. I'm part of those plans. I don't think it hurts that Daddy threw a bunch of money at them, and my brother, Nate, offered to let us use Time Out for some big fundraising get-togethers. Thank god he owns the place. But it's a job. I'm just glad I don't have to go back to Great Falls and live with my parents."

"Brick wouldn't have liked that," Avery added.

"Yeah, well after you moved out, I wasn't sure I'd have much choice."

Avery had moved out of the apartment she shared with Nat after graduation. She would have left sooner, but she wanted to wait until she graduated. Jacob asked her to move in with him the day they let her out of the hospital. It had taken her days to convince him it was a bad idea while she was still in school. Fortunately, she had Luke backing her up, as well as Charles Ross's directive to keep things low-key. Jacob had reluctantly agreed.

Avery narrowed her eyes and gave her friend a playful glare. "I doubt that. Brick was pretty much moved in by the time I left. I had to step over his beer bottles to get out the door."

Nat rolled her eyes. "Not all of us live with the perfect man."

Avery didn't like the tone of Nat's voice. It wasn't jealousy; it was something else. "Natasha, what's wrong?"

Nat glanced around the coffee shop then pointed at the door. "Speak of the devil. Perfect man headed this way." She snatched up her backpack and rose to her feet. "I'll see you later." She gave Avery a hug and mumbled "hello" to Jacob as she headed out the door.

Jacob slipped into the booth beside Avery and slid his arm around her waist. "Hey, sweetheart. How you holding up?"

"Okay." She rested her head on his shoulder. "I'm glad it's over. Or mostly over, I guess."

He kissed the top of her head and hugged her close. "I feel like I can't apologize enough."

"Yeah, well, you need to knock it off," Avery quipped. "You need to stop blaming yourself for what Brent did. He's off his rocker, living in his own reality that doesn't include the truth in any way, shape, or form. I thought he was my friend, and he was trying to help us. You didn't know he was obsessive and crazy any more than I did."

"If we hadn't been dating—"

"He would have still done it," she interrupted. "It wouldn't have mattered if I was dating you or not. It would have happened either way. And if it wasn't for you, no one would have known Brent took me, and who knows what would have happened. I owe you my life."

Jacob rested his forehead on hers. "I love you, Ms. Collins."

Avery wrapped a hand around the back of his neck and brushed a kiss across his lips.

"I love you too, Professor Moore."

The End

Author Bio

Mimi Francis is a northern girl living in the much warmer southwest with no intention of going back. She's always been a voracious reader and ever since she was a little girl, stories played in her head, daydreams she turned into intricate stories. It took her more than forty years to put pen to paper and start writing, but she hasn't looked back since. Once her three children grew up and started their own lives, she decided it was time to chase her dreams and she's been running after them ever since.

She loves writing contemporary, romantic fiction because it's fun to write about people letting themselves go and getting down and dirty with someone that makes their blood boil. Mimi stumbled into writing when she started writing fanfiction for her favorite obsessions. People loved her stories, so she grabbed the reins and barreled headlong into writing original fiction.

When she's not busy writing, Mimi loves to binge-watch new shows, fawn over her favorite Supernatural monster hunters, rewatch her collection of Marvel movies, crochet, and spend time with her husband and their dogs.

Mimi wants to give readers an escape, even if it's just for a little bit, a chance to get away from their everyday lives and be transported into a world of romance with a lot of erotic fun thrown into it.

You can find her at mimifrancis.com or on Instagram and Facebook @author.mimi.francis

4 Horsemen Publications

Romance

Ann Shepphird
The War Council

Emily Bunney
All or Nothing
All the Way
All Night Long: Novella
All She Needs
Having it All
All at Once
All Together
All for Her

Lynn Chantale
The Baker's Touch
Blind Secrets

Mimi Francis
Private Lives
Private Protection
Run Away Home
The Professor

Fantasy & Paranormal Romance

Beau Lake
The Beast Beside Me
The Beast Within Me
Taming the Beast: Novella
The Beast After Me
Charming the Beast: Novella
The Beast Like Me
An Eye for Emeralds
Swimming in Sapphires
Pining for Pearls

D. Lambert
To Walk into the Sands
Rydan
Celebrant
Northlander
Esparan
King
Traitor
His Last Name

J.M. Paquette
Klauden's Ring
Solyn's Body
The Inbetween
Hannah's Heart
Call Me Forth
Invite Me In

Lyre R. Saenz
Prelude
Falsetto in the Woods: Novella
Ragtime Swing
Sonata
Song of the Sea
The Devil's Trill
Bercuese
To Heal a Songbird
Ghost March
Nocturne

4HorsemenPublications.com